# BEAUTIFUL/GROTESQUE

EDITED BY SAM RICHARD

# CONTENTS

# INTRODUCTION
## SAM RICHARD

When I first saw this Untitled 1968 illustration (see previous page) from renowned Polish artist Zdzisław Beksiński, I knew immediately that I wanted to figure out how to use it for cover art on a Weirdpunk release (unfortunately the image is too small). Like all his work, it's so evocative and striking. Unlike most of his work that he seems to be most known for, it appears to just be pencil and paper, though I'm no art historian so don't quote me on that.

Through a couple of twists and turns, the piece ultimately became a launching point for the book you are now reading. The illustration crawled under my skin in that perfect way that art often does, and it inspired me to ask Weirdpunk alumni and friends Jo Quenell, Katy Michelle Quinn, Joanna Koch, and Roland Blackburn if they would like to join me in creating a mini-anthology with the simple theme of "beautiful/grotesque."

That was it. In whatever way the author decided to interpret that concept, I was looking for them to write a short story that captured that feeling. Much like Jo, Katy, and I had previously done with the Filthy Loot mini-anthology *Lazermall*, the idea was to see what we could each come up with from a singular focal point.

What strikes me most is how differently we all interpreted the loose prompt. Yes, there is some thematic overlap here, but the tones and atmospheres, the types of stories told, are all so different. Some are on the quieter end of horror, while others go full extreme horror, some are more fun while others are somber. And yet all fully grasp the initial idea.

I need to thank the contributing authors for saying yes to this hare-brained idea I randomly had. I love the varied ways they all interpreted the prompt and the book is so strong due to their talent. I'm honored to have such amazing and talented friends. It's my hope that 2021 and beyond will see more Weirdpunk releases that are in this mini-anthology vein, so think of this book as a launching point for more cool small projects.

Also, thank you for picking up this strange little experiment we all took part in. I hope you find it worth your while, even as uncomfortable or unnerving as it may be at times; or perhaps because of that.

# GOD OF THE SILVERED HALLS
## - ROLAND BLACKBURN

A lot of bodies had found their way to her over the years, but Patience was still surprised when she opened the drawer.

*Just when you thought you'd seen everything.*

"Looks like a train wreck," Larry offered, slipping up beside her with a magician's grace. It would be a win if he didn't drip sandwich on the corpse.

Sighing, Patience circled around the big man, always careful not to touch him, for a closer look. Brushing a limp lock of hair out of her eyes, she examined the body, the wound.

To her disappointment, he wasn't wrong.

The young woman in the stainless steel drawer was a study in alabaster from the waist up. High cheekbones, aquiline nose, with shock of black hair surrounding her like a princess from a fairy tale. Her skin was flawless ivory, from her delicate neck and dainty collarbone to what could only be considered perfect breasts. From the waist down, however—

Pride wasn't a virtue, but Patience had earned it after twenty years in the medical examiner's office. She wasn't about to get sick, especially in front of Larry. "Put the sandwich down and get the camera."

"My shift hasn't started."

"I already logged you in."

The big man glanced back at the battered computer on their shared desk. "I don't know if I like you knowing my password."

"Then don't move your lips when you type. I'm sure you can come up with something better, *prettykitty69*."

Larry grinned. "We're going to do this one tonight?"

"Fuck no, Larry. I've got plans." Patience didn't, but the thought of spending another three hours on a trauma victim with a side of oafish leering sent chills through her, even in the refrigerated room. Between the walls of silvered metal, she caught a glimpse of herself and shuddered, a skeletal bird-thing in a white lab coat.

*What happened to you?*

"Huh. No overtime?"

"The dead aren't exactly piling up. Kudlow would have my ass."

With a petulant shrug, Larry did as he was told. For a big man, he moved like an acrobat. Tossing down his hoagie and rummaging through the filing cabinet for the digital camera, Larry's sneakers barely whispered on the hard tile.

Once more alone, Patience leaned closer to the body

to escape her own infinite reflections, and that was when she spotted it.

A tattoo, starting at the woman's ribcage and licking down between navel and hip, or at least where the hip would have been. The corpse had been bisected, ragged flaps of gore hanging gently against the milk-white skin. Only a ruinous hollow now existed, the barest fist of glistening spine jutting through.

The black design arcing down her side was a whorl of artistic calligraphy.

Larry almost jostled her onto the body on his way back, then caught himself, barely managing to avoid wrenching the morgue drawer off the track. The fact that he was doing a bit annoyed her, but she followed her role and danced nimbly out of his way, snatching up the clipboard.

ODOT had found her, as Larry had suggested, by the train tracks off of Columbia. Torn in half beneath the shadows of a decrepit industrial park.

*Lucille Malten. D.O.B. 12-17-39.*

*That can't be right.*

"Hey, check out this ink!" Larry boomed, swinging the camera towards her. The morgue was wide, with more than enough room for an examination table, two people, and the drawers to be open on both sides, but Larry always found a way to be on top of her. "You went to medical school."

"Years ago, Larry."

"What does it say?"

Patience peered past him, taking in the Latin for just

a fraction longer than was necessary. Maybe she'd finally seen everything.

"It's a recipe."

**P**erched at the end of the bar, Patience sipped her gin-and-tonic and kept one eye on the door. Every breath she took held the faintest odor of formaldehyde, an idea which she knew couldn't be true but still persisted. Her phone rested on the battered hardwood like a docile insect.

For the hundredth time that night, she wondered how she'd gotten there.

Her gaze flickered up to the mirror behind the scarred counter, and she quickly quashed that. All she needed right now was the sight of her, the living corpse of the bright young thing she'd once been. She already recognized herself for what she was: a ghoul that preyed upon the chattel, cutting and tearing and weighing and sawing ever onwards, right on into that great abyss.

*Jeez, but you need to get laid.*

But that was just it. She didn't. The idea of someone else touching her was physically nauseating. Any person that would have her, would accept her for what she was, could only be a twisted reflection of herself.

She'd sooner tear her heart out with the shard of mirror across the bar.

*If Danny hadn't died--*

But she'd been down that road before, and it was two gin-and-tonics too early for maudlin.

He had, of course, and in grand fashion. Why he'd done it was another question entirely, but that hadn't stopped him from washing up in one of her drawers a decade ago, a bloated pale thing three days in the river.

There had never been a note. Just a sudden and profound hole in her life that she liked to fill in the early hours of the morning, theories and connections interweaving into a collective mannequin of motive and inner life. Just before dawn, she liked to think he'd been pushed.

Patience couldn't quite bring herself to believe it.

She waved over the curvy woman in the black t-shirt who'd just taken over, signaling for another.

The bartender looked at her concoction doubtfully. "People still drink those?"

"I do."

"Jeez. You and my grandmother. On the house, then."

Too tired to rebuke her, Patience instead scanned the ill-lit bar. A half-dozen regulars were buried in their cups, a trio of hipsters shooting pool on the worn table in back. She caught her own eyes in the mirror again and tore them away, but not before she got another good look at the face staring back at her.

She barely recognized it.

The circles under her eyes, her limp hair. The wrinkles that had crept in when she hadn't been looking.

Not monstrous, she knew. Just—other.

*What the hell happened to you?*

Her phone buzzed against the hardwood, and she scooped it up without enthusiasm. It was Hector, the final nail in the coffin of her celibacy. She was late on his spousal support, she knew, but couldn't bring herself to give the parasite another rasher of blood until she absolutely had to. He had been a poor imitation of Danny, a mask that had slipped far too soon—

*Enough.*

She killed the vibrations and pumped in her password, searching for a distraction to pull her out of this wallow. Her drink was in her hand, bitter gin passing her lips without flavor.

The photo came up at once.

Too worn out to blush, a delicious tickle of guilt nonetheless coursed through her.

She knew she shouldn't have taken the risk.

Shouldn't have taken the picture.

Knew that if Larry had turned around a moment sooner, he would finally have that shot at the top spot he'd been coveting for years. But she had been—

*—compelled—*

—fascinated by the immaculate cadaver, half in the steel drawer and half who-knows-where. For the first time, she wondered what might have happened to her.

*What could do that to a person?*

She thought of what it must have been like, to lie down on those cold tracks in the dead of night. To feel the rumble of the approaching engine, the gnashing of tectonic plates, and to not lose your nerve.

Patience was almost jealous.

That design, though. The spiral of black ink, sweeping curves and sharp-edged characters, ebbing downwards into that single scrap of flesh, dangling into a gory terminus.

It sank its talons into her eye, refusing to let go.

She had never understood tattooing. Establishing permanence in this whirling, rotting maelstrom had always felt a lie.

*What is given, kids, can be taken away.*

*The fucking story of my life.*

But the significance of it. What it may have meant to the exquisite corpse filled her mind, an abject curiosity that began to overwhelm her.

Moreover, what did it create?

**T**his is stupid.

Like many people with the same thought, she never stopped moving.

Patience was feeling it as she pulled out old spices and random ingredients from the cupboard above the stove. Her balance had faded, each gesture now a lurch that threatened to send her toppling to the floor. A box of pinot was half-dead in the old refrigerator she'd been thinking of trading out for the last six months.

Lately even her blurred reflection in the polished door was becoming too much.

The tattoo didn't call for anything complicated. She would have frozen if it had, given up all this macabre cookery as an intoxicated whimsy and put herself to bed. But everything she needed was already lying about the apartment, either in the desiccated contents of the fridge or buried in the spice rack of one-and-done purchases that were probably a dozen years old or more.

*Well, not* everything--

That last inked word was hard to determine, irregular and left dangling by a thread of sinew. What it commanded was out of the question, clearly.

The nagging question returned.

*Why would someone have this tattooed on their midsection?*

Slamming down the dregs of her wine and wiping her mouth with the back of one hand, Patience was about to find out.

*This is stupid.*

She dolloped the ingredients into the blender, one by one, her measurements canted and overflowing. Coriander. Cinnamon. Anise. Nutmeg. A half-dozen others, none of whose flavors she surmised should ever be combined. Five hundred years ago, the recipe would have meant a voyage across the East Indies and cost a fortune.

Today, about thirty bucks and a trip to Krogers.

Two eggs cracked against the glass. A trip to the medicine cabinet retrieved the homeopathic alkaloid tablets Hector had scammed her into buying for his frequent stomach upsets. Maybe guilt had been twisting him even then, for all the good it had done her.

Besides, it wasn't like she could just buy raw belladonna alongside the vitamins.

Unboxing another glass of wine, she cast a doubtful eye upon the contents of the jar. A spiral of muted colors, suspended in meaty ether.

Without another thought, Patience hit *puree*. Blades whirred to life.

At this hour, the maelstrom seemed much too loud for her tiny apartment.

The alabaster goddess rose to the forefront of her mind, dreaming in cold steel as Patience watched the mixture froth, subdued colors coalescing into a brown sludge.

*You wouldn't think you could be jealous of a corpse.*

After a few minutes and the last of the pinot, she stopped the machine's infernal whirring and popped the lid off, surveying the contents.

By all appearances, the tattoo appeared to create the world's most noxious protein shake.

Something cloying hit the back of her sinuses, a clinging mixture of musk and meaty incense that called to mind old tombs and lost liaisons. Her pulse quickened.

She swallowed nervously.

Just looking into the blender made her gorge rise.

*You're not actually going to--*

*The fuck you aren't.*

In one quick burst she hoisted the jar to her lips and let the mixture ooze across her tongue, crawling coyly down her throat. It clung to her mouth with ancient talons, choked her, filling her with a dull warmth.

The room began to lose focus, canting drunkenly onto one axis.

Patience forced the concoction down in three long gulps, trying to ignore the grotesque gamy-sweet flavor that was invading her nostrils. Her other hand clutched the counter in a death grip as she began to sweat.

Finally, she dropped the glass, barely hitting the sink.

She urged herself not to be sick--

*--What were you thinking WHAT WERE YOU THINKING--*

--but then the nauseous urge was gone, just as quickly as it had come.

Muttering, she drained another half glass of wine from the box in the refrigerator and chugged it, trying to wash the aftertaste away. Already the memory of flavor was fading, an afterthought that was somehow hollowing, a peculiar longing for malaise.

Patience wondered what would take its place.

When the refrigerator door slammed shut, she once more averted her eyes from her reflection. In less than five minutes, the rest of the wine was gone, and Patience was snoring dully on the couch, her mind having finally given up the ghost.

In her dreams, the pallid vision in the drawer rolled over.

And smiled.

"Three dead bodies are delivered to the mortuary, right? And each of them has a big smile on their face--"

"I don't have time for this, Larry. Get your side."

The big man frowned but subsided, the pair of them shifting the corpse onto the examination table. "Come on. For someone in such a shitty mood, you *look* happier than you have in weeks."

"Don't make me write you up." Patience allowed herself to breathe as she clicked on the recorder. Mild hangover notwithstanding, she'd awoken with a pang in her gut that even a fast-food breakfast couldn't quell. Maybe that was part of the problem.

Seeing the dead woman relieved her, if only for a moment.

*The alabaster goddess.*

*We're about to burn down her temple.*

"Come on, smile. This is the biggest waste of time we've had this year." Larry fumbled at the clipboard. "Who is this chick, anyway?"

"*Lucille Malten.*" Patience intoned, speaking more for posterity than anyone else in the room. "*D.O.B. 12-17-39. Apparent birth date error in the paperwork, with the nine and three reversed. Subject is Caucasian woman in their mid-twenties. Apparent cause of death is extreme piercing trauma resulting in the severing of the lower body between the C3 and C4 vertebrae. Said lower body, including the sacrum, pelvic girdle, and both legs has not been recovered and is currently missing. Injury effected massive blood loss, severe intestinal damage, apparent organ loss.*"

Wielding the scalpel, Patience caught a glimpse of herself in the mirrored wall and turned away, a ghoul caught out in the light. Her hand hovered above the ivory flesh of the woman's chest, a strange tremble in her grasp that she hoped Larry didn't notice.

She took a deep breath to steady herself, eyes drifting down to the whorl of ink cascading down the corpse's right side. That last word--

*--the last ingredient--*

Patience brought the blade down, hurrying through the Y-incision, cutting deep below the pale corpse's breasts before drawing a deep line down to the pubic bone. What little gore remained was only a dried frosting. Holding her breath, she peeled back the soft tissue into three neat flaps.

It was like kicking in a stained glass window.

"You okay, boss?" Larry asked.

"I'm fine," she murmured, forcing on a smile. With a burst of inspiration, she handed him the blade. "Like you said. This is a waste of time."

Larry recoiled as if she was about to shank him. She grinned wider, exposing all of her teeth. "I've got a bunch of paperwork to burn through. You want to do the honors?"

Taking the scalpel, the big man flashed her a completely inappropriate smile, tugged at his collar, and began. As he began detaching the remaining organs with aplomb, weighing them, slicing away tissue samples for review and calling out his findings for posterity, he was so wrapped up in his element—

*—his big break—*

—that he hadn't noticed that Patience hadn't budged. She'd only wrapped her arms around herself, backing up against the ice-cold silvered drawers for support.

She didn't want to look away. Far from it.

Her eyes kept being drawn to that rogue flap of skin, the whorl of ink.

Right above where the hip should be.

*—that last ingredient—*

A low rumble came from somewhere within her. Patience realized that she was licking her lips.

Larry removed the body block and slipped it behind the corpse's neck like a macabre pillow. Ignoring the whir of the electric saw as it started up, she caught a glimpse of herself again in the stainless steel lockers. What she saw stopped her cold.

It was only a flicker, she told herself. Not real at all.

Forcing herself to move, she flopped down in the chair behind the shared desk, careful not to actually touch herself with the gore-streaked latex gloves as the room began a slow rotation. Something groaned within her, and she peeled the latex off, dropping them inside-out onto the cluttered laminate. Larry maintained the pace of his recordable litany as Patience ran an awkward hand through her surprisingly lush hair, fingers trembling.

*Get a hold of yourself.*

*This isn't you.*

Taking a deep breath, Patience hunched over and logged into the battered PC, getting her password right on the third try. For the next hour, she busied herself distractedly with the odds and ends of bureaucracy, trying to ignore the whirring wet sounds coming from across the room as the beautiful stranger was reduced to the sum of their parts.

At last, she gave up trying to ignore it.

Snatching a new pair of gloves from a cardboard box, she pocketed the inside-out pair, unwilling to admit to herself what she was about to do. She crossed the mirrored room in five long strides, averting her eyes from the burnished walls, gnashing ghouls reflecting to infinity. Patience kept her gaze trained on the ruined body before her.

What had been alabaster was now a mess of pink

and red.

Larry didn't even register her arrival, face-down with a microscope and tissue sample. She glanced down at the table. Organs glistened in the glaring overhead light.

On impulse, she seized the scalpel off of the examination table. "How's it going?

He never even looked up. "Great. Just great."

"Yeah?" She sidled a little closer, slipping between Larry and the exposed viscera. Her eyes lifted to the flap of skin, wrenched away and dangling near the lip of the island. Even inverted, she still felt the whorl of ink, the crafted letters spelling out the only thing she needed.

*That last word, most of all.*

"Yeah." Larry raised his eyes, and she tucked the blade behind her back. "I mean, half her internal organs are missing. Probably scattered across the next dozen miles of tracks or splattered across the cow-catcher of whatever hit her. Whatever was left, though, shows elevated levels of progesterone. Chorionic gonadotropin."

"She was pregnant?"

"That's just it. From the rest of the body, I don't think so. There's no other signs that she was carrying something inside her."

The big man stood and ambled over to the body. "You've been doing this a lot longer than I have. Tell me what you see."

He gestured to the skin flaps, the outer edges of what had been the epidermis and muscle. Surprised by his sudden deference, Patience played along.

"By only a visual? The soft tissue was bisected by an

irregular tool, most likely through high-velocity impact. The edges aren't neat but ragged, suggesting trauma rather than deliberation."

Larry almost ran a hand through his hair, then noticed his bloody gloves and thought better of it. "Yeah. But something doesn't jibe here. I'm going to look a little more into it."

There was a question at the end, subordinate to ordinate. "Of course. Take your time."

He grinned. "Ok. You really do look like you're feeling better."

The big man turned and shuffled back over to the microscope.

Recognizing what she needed on the counter, Patience took a deep breath and held it.

Once Larry put his eye to the lens, she tensed.

*This is insane.*

*You'll lose your job. Or worse.*

Turning, the scalpel sung in a sweet, soft arc, a dart of silver parting muscle and sinew like raw butter. Patience glanced up, fully expecting Larry to be gawking at her in horror, but he hummed, still engrossed in whatever the hell he thought he was finding.

She snatched the gobbet of meat between her latex-covered fingers and tucked it neatly into the inside-out glove in her pocket.

*The last ingredient.*

*What could it hurt to try?*

Her stomach rumbled.

S he didn't look up until the bartender said something.

"Shit, girl. Whatever you been doing, it's working."

Patience showed her teeth again before she realized the compliment was genuine. "Thanks."

It had been a frenzied drive back to her apartment, the contraband burning a hole in her pocket until she could get inside and lock the door behind her. She'd held the glistening morsel before her, a raw red lump, before depositing it in the blender with the rest of the ingredients like an infernal margarita.

*What mysteries lie within the human heart?*

*Tasty ones, it turns out.*

This time, the mixture had a meaty pungency, the taste of sacrificial altars. Temples left to rot.

It had been heavenly.

She had no idea what consuming this might say about her. Only that Patience was already regretting not procuring more.

The bartender nodded back, their sage work apparently done, and sidled on down the bar to wait on the trio of hipsters shooting pool. Their absence left Patience with an unobscured view of the mirror behind them, and, preparing to wince, she caught a glimpse of herself.

For a moment, she forgot to breathe.

It wasn't so much that she was unrecognizable. Far from it. But the change--

*The change.*

Patience had woken up that morning a pert and lively fifty-two years old. She'd had to admit that she'd felt better than she had in years, an extra bounce to her hair, a glint in her eyes, the slackening skin somehow made more radiant and taut. But this—

The circles and furrows had receded. The wrinkles and crows' feet likewise. Her sagging flesh clung tighter than it had in years.

*You're five years younger. Easily.*

*Also a cannibal. But who's counting?*

Her phone buzzed against the hardwood. Hector again. She let it die.

*If this was what one full recipe could do—*

Something deep inside her growled.

She welcomed it.

A weight settled on the stool next to her, and a gravely voice began a sales pitch in her ear as old as bars themselves. Without turning her head, she dismissed the voice curtly, but her heart began to race.

*When was the last time someone gave you even that?*

For a moment, she considered the alabaster goddess, the half-form peeled apart and locked away behind the silvered walls. Born in '39. Maybe it hadn't been a typo after all.

But then, how would *she* have found it?

The voice, when it came, was from over her shoulder. "Ma'am? You need another one of those?"

Patience looked down. Her gin and tonic had reduced itself to watery dregs.

The voice belonged to one of the hipster kids, full beard and black-rimmed glasses under a wool cap the color of dead forests. If this had been five minutes ago, she'd have assumed they were making fun of her. But now--

She felt her old power returning, something beginning to fill that hollow where her life had been.

"Sure," she purred. "Maybe two."

※

"Someone's been eating their Quaker Oats."

"New skin cream, Larry. I guess it's working." Patience drummed her fingers on the examination table. "What was it you had to show me?"

"What? Oh, yeah." The big man peeled his eyes off her and slid gracefully over to the desk, snatching up a clipboard with an illusionist's grace. Patience felt her attention drawn to the thirteenth drawer, to the vivisected goddess within it waiting to be claimed. She could picture her, beating against the walls with fleshy wings, a dark butterfly gone to rot.

*Please let it still be there. Please.*

A cloud of dark spots crowded the edges of her vision, and Patience rubbed them away. She hadn't been sleeping well lately, or truth be told, a lot. Her reflection stared back at her in the burnished wall, a lively thing now, bright and full of mischief.

If she still saw the ghoul beneath, well--

*That's to be expected, right?*

"Here." Larry found what he was looking for, thrusting the clipboard towards her.

Patience didn't understand what she was supposed to

be seeing. "High velocity trauma. We've been over this, Larry."

He sighed. "You're looking at it backwards."

"I don't think so."

"I don't think it was a train." The big man swallowed, gathering his resolve. Patience didn't like the grave expression crowding his sallow features, his fleshiness trying to gain poise. "The edges of the wound are all wrong. The suppuration begins from the soft tissue and radiates outwards to the epidermis."

She waited. Larry didn't disappoint. "Something tore her apart. Maybe from the inside."

Patience was dumbstruck. He took this as acceptance. "Or whoever did this pierced her through a tiny incision, expanded a hook, then pulled. Or used a back-hoe. Or some industrial—shit, I don't know. All I'm saying is that this was deliberate. I think someone bisected her, dumped the body at the tracks, and hoped we'd think train. We almost did."

Gathering herself, Patience nodded. "I'll double check your work, but good job. You've really hung onto this one."

He beamed. "Thanks, boss."

"Has the victim been claimed yet?"

"That was the other thing. We got a hold of her next of kin, a nephew out of Sarasota, this morning. They requested that she be incinerated. No delay."

It took a moment for his words to sink in. *Why are you so slow today?* "Wait—past tense?"

"Matthieu took care of it this morning." Larry

nodded at the sagging file cabinet. "Manilla envelope. Third from the bottom."

Something inside her screamed.

*The recipe.*

*No, fuck that. The heart.*

But that was fruitless. Patience just needed to take a breath and calm down. The dark spots were back, swarming at the edges of her vision, but she waved them away with an impatient hand.

She had made a hard copy of the photo.

Several in fact, just in case something were to happen to her phone.

As for hearts, well--

If the recipe couldn't function without the alabaster woman's, she was screwed. But if that was the case, eventually she would have been anyway.

*But if it does work--*

It wasn't like the county morgue had a shortage of donors.

As long as she was discreet, no one need ever know.

She just had to keep cutting.

"Who's on the docket for today?"

W eeks passed.
They'd stopped recognizing her at the local watering hole, which suited Patience just fine. High on her perch now, she could pass for a woman in her late twenties, and the years just kept sliding off.

She'd tried the recipe six times, having stolen two

more hearts; one from a teen whose skateboard hadn't been a match for the bus and another from a middle-aged man who'd had a nasty experience with a blender gone bad. All the remaining viscera had been incinerated. Neither would be missed.

And Patience—well—

Finishing another gin and tonic at the edge of the bar, she glanced around her kingdom. The same half-dozen regulars were in the pews, eyes now glued to her ass. The three hipsters lounged at the far end, feigning at playing pool and pretending not to ogle her.

The wrinkles and lines were almost gone, her flesh returned to supple. Patience felt amazing.

Patience felt hungry.

But she could live with that. She could live with the black spots that sometimes crossed her vision, the result of long nights and troubled dreams. In time, she'd be able to rest again.

The occasional rumbling within her was easily quenched, even if she wanted the recipe more and more often. She'd every intention of feeding it.

Now and forever.

But every so often, when she found her reflection, she thought she could catch a glimpse of something. Something moving.

A pale ripple, just below her skin, and always gone when she studied harder or looked again.

*The ghoul within you.*

*Just fighting its way to the surface.*

*A manifestation of guilt. Somewhere deep down, you don't think you deserve this, not even after all you suffered.*

*Why are the pretty ones always insane?*

She signaled for another gin-and-tonic, enjoying how the bartender hurried now.

Oh, she couldn't keep this up forever. She knew that. When she hit her early twenties—

—*let's be real*—

—her late teens, there were going to be some questions asked. The kind that didn't have any easy answers.

People would balk at the prom queen who claimed thirty years' experience in forensic pathology. There was just no getting around that.

But she didn't care. Doors that had shut so long ago were opening again. No more Hector. No sad, lost Danny. No more tragic little ghoul, afraid to catch a glimpse of herself amidst the silvered walls. She could take her meager savings and start over somewhere.

Somewhere—fun.

The world was going to be hers again.

All she had to do was take it.

And feed.

"Some skin cream, huh?"

Patience froze mid-autopsy. The scalpel dipped beneath the lip of the table, just out of sight. "I thought you went home."

"You thought what I wanted you to." The big man slipped from the doorway, flopping down behind their shared desk, the beaten PC dangerously close to one elbow. He was clad only in a t-shirt and jeans, some alchemical symbol plastered across the front of the cotton. For once he looked, well—normal.

Everything, maybe, except for the sneer. "But I mean it. You look amazing. Who would have thought?"

The corpse before her had its mahogany skin stretched to three points on the compass, chest cavity completely exposed. Arrayed before her on the table were a host of organs.

Only one had any real significance anymore.

Conspicuously absent, that one was tucked neatly away in a Ziploc bag, now at the bottom of her purse.

"Thanks, I guess—" she began, but Larry cut her off.

"After-hours autopsy, huh? I thought there was no overtime."

Patience sighed, her fingernails drumming on the steel table through her latex gloves. Half-obscured by the ruin of the body, it was no great trick to make the surgical steel disappear.

Larry folded his arms across his chest, a half-assed Poirot. "I bet you're wondering how I found out."

She almost tried to feign ignorance, a *found out what, Larry?*, but she was too tired to care. "No, not really."

He seemed disappointed. "Oh."

For a moment, she thought he was going to go on with his grand monologue anyway, but he appeared to think better of it. "I don't know what Brazilian doctor or black-arts medical college you're stealing for in exchange for your wonder cream, but it ends now."

"Yeah?" It sounded stupid coming out of her mouth, but for once she was at an acerbic loss for words.

"Yeah."

She sighed, offering him her profile. In her past life, it has been an a-bomb in her arsenal. "What is it you want, Larry?"

"Your spot. Resign. Go your own way with whatever this is, and I won't report any of it to Kudlow."

"Report what?" She took a deep breath, letting her chest press against the fabric of the smock. "What exactly is it you're accusing me of?"

"You're stealing organs. For someone or something." He looked poised to take a celebratory lap around the room. "No one notices because the entrails get inciner-ated afterwards. But if I was to do an inventory of every-thing laid out in front of you, I wouldn't find the heart.

"You're sick, Patience. You've always been sick. And since you milf-ed out, it's just gotten worse."

"So, I step down." Patience almost laughed. "And then what? You take the top spot?"

He bristled. "I've done my time."

"You're not qualified. Getting rid of me isn't going to get you what you want. It sure won't get me what I want." Patience leaned over the exam table, pushing her chest out. It was a hard trick not to smear herself with viscera. "But maybe we can come to some kind of other-arrangement?"

"I'm gay." Larry scowled. "You really were a terrible boss."

She shrugged, catching a glimpse of herself in the stainless steel drawers that lined the room.

*Nothing below the surface.* "Fine. I'm going."

"Really?" The big man pushed himself back from the desk. "I mean, you'd better."

"Just let me get my things." She crossed the room in five quick strides, kneeling down by Larry's feet to grab her bag. The big man didn't move, only let her supplicate herself before him.

The scalpel was out like a gift.

F rom her throne in the dive bar, Patience was glowing.

It hadn't been hard to make Larry disappear. Not when she had access to industrial-grade surgical tools, a crematory, and the password to his county email account. Two vitriol-laced tirades to Kudlow and a completed timecard were all it took to dissolve his employment, and the Columbia had swallowed his car as easily as a dream.

They hadn't gotten around to hiring a replacement yet. Patience had the morgue all to herself, an empress amidst silvered halls.

All heads were half-turned towards her; a radiant thing that couldn't possibly survive being carded. Her solitude amongst the dead had unsurprisingly not led to her scaling back.

The lines were gone. So were the wrinkles. Her flesh was as supple and pert as it had been when she was accepting her high school diploma.

All those doors, wide open again.

Patience had never felt more alive. She had a nasty feeling that she might be paying Hector a visit soon.

*You can never collect enough hearts.*

Sure, she couldn't sleep. The dark spots that dotted

her vision, the uncomfortable glimpses in the mirror of something moving beneath her skin: these had only increased over time. But gone was the revulsion at her own reflection, the cowering at what she had become.

One of the hipsters set a gin-and-tonic before her, then scurried away.

If any of the county higher-ups could be bothered to come down to the morgue, they'd think it a bring-your-daughter-to-work day.

As it was, she just had to hope no one ever bothered to check the freezer in her apartment.

A cloud of black wasps drifted across her eyes, and she shuddered, wondering if fatigue alone could really account for it. Sometimes it felt like something else was behind her gaze, looking out at the world with a dull but dawning comprehension.

*If you left the morgue behind, stopped taking the recipe, what would happen?*

She wasn't sure. It didn't seem like she could just age through her years normally, a new lease on life purchased right off the lot.

More likely, she would begin to rot.

*Or worse.*

For the first time in weeks, her thoughts turned to the alabaster goddess, the half-form now so much ash on the wind. Clearly, she'd taken the recipe to heart, so to speak. Eighty-years-old with the body of a lingerie model. Was this how she had felt? If only Patience could have asked her—

*—how she was torn apart. Remember? The crime they never solved—*

That thought was an errant fly, and Patience swatted it without mercy. She wasn't invulnerable; she had no illusions about that. The goddess had come to a bad end. Beyond that—

It was an ugly question, and she only had time for the beautiful.

Something inside her rumbled.

She rose and strutted over to the pool table. A dozen heads turned to watch her go.

The three hipsters were huddled around a deficient bartop, nervously nursing their tall cans of PBR. They didn't play much pool anymore. No one in the dive bar did much of anything.

A cloud of dark matter flirted across her eyes. She ignored it.

"Worship me," she said.

In the red light, they fell to their knees.

Patience sighed. As long as she had the harvest of the silvered hall, the world was hers.

She intended to keep it that way.

Young blood notwithstanding, Patience shivered between the mirrored walls.

A middle-aged woman splayed dead on the table before her, with two more stocked away in the drawers to either side, envelopes of meat she hadn't rifled through yet. Playing with her hair, time to kill, Patience let the vibrant silk lock flit between her fingers.

It had been getting a little hard to concentrate lately.

Patience wondered if that was a side effect of youth or the recipe.

Like so many other things lately, she decided it didn't matter.

Without Larry, being in a refrigerated room surrounded by the dead was actually getting a little tedious. Not for the first time, she contemplated moving on, finding something fresh and exciting and, well—young.

Hollywood, even.

There was more than one way to take a heart.

But Kudlow was sending Larry's replacement over this morning. Failing to receive any sort of background information other than the name Lindsey, Patience had no idea what to expect, only that she supposed to be on standby. The morning would be full of orientation and some on-the-job training once they arrived.

She wondered how they'd handle the work. If maybe they'd be sick.

*Who knows?*

*Maybe a little fresh meat'll liven things up.*

Faced with the tedium, she hummed, cycling through the drawers. Inventory had always been Larry's task, and she realized that since his—well, repurposing, she'd never done a thorough walkthrough, only glanced at the clipboards left piled on the desk.

The thirteenth drawer was ajar.

Just a crack.

Frowning, she crossed the room and peeled it open.

The room began to spin slowly around her. Something clutched in her chest.

*Should you have known he was just fucking with you?*
*Had he known, even then?*

On a burnished platter, the alabaster goddess was the gory sum of her parts. Beneath the milk-white skin was a red ruin that Larry had barely bothered to reassemble. Glassy eyes stared back at her from beneath the horizontal slit of a broken cranium.

Patience's mouth began to water.

She picked up the scalpel.

A dark hive crowded the edges of her vision, a cloud of nightmare swarming against the mirrored walls. Patience stared back at her reflection, at the vibrant blur of her new life amongst the dead, then took the scrap she wanted.

Only hanging on by a thread, it was hers with a flick of the wrist.

Holding the tatter up to the florescent light, she read the calligraphic whorls again, kneading the loose skin beneath her fingers.

Without thinking, Patience put it in her mouth and chewed.

She would burn her predecessor's remains, scatter them to the four winds.

She would be left the sole inheritor, a black spider on a carrion web.

The god of the silvered halls.

But as she swallowed, something rumbled inside her.

This time, it did not cease.

A massive weight shifted inside her, and Patience threw up one arm, bracing herself against the icy drawer, staggering to one knee.

Without warning, the region just below her navel seized in anguish, draping a sheet of cold agony across her that annihilated her nerve endings. It was a piercing unlike anything she had ever felt before. Had ever thought she could feel.

Something terrible was clawing at her midsection, tearing, gnawing. Trying to find a way out.

When the fingers peeled her muscle back, she couldn't even scream.

Patience could only watch as the ebon hands erupted through the flesh of her midriff in an obscene parody of birth, then pressed. Blood coursed from the gaping wound as it even now stretched, and stretched--

Her legs gave way, dumping Patience on her ass as the thing inside her found purchase and really began to shove, dark talons carving the tear in her midsection into a wet red line. The reek of copper and spoiled meat assaulted her sinuses. A black form was visible, just beneath the surface of her pulsing viscera.

Head lolling with the waves of anguish, fingers clenching uselessly against the blood-slicked tile, Patience found herself face to face with the remnants of the alabaster goddess.

The corpse's pale eyes flapped open, a ruined smile across her blasted features.

In this black epiphany, Patience understood.

The thing inside her gave one more colossal shrug, and Patience felt herself let go. Muscle tore almost to the small of her back, sending dark things slipping from her torso and skittering across the linoleum. Everything was now shadow and silver and scarlet.

Graceless, the dark shape emerged from her, humanoid.

Growing.

It took its first tottering steps to the alabaster goddess and began to feed.

Patience slid down the mirrored wall, at once hot and growing colder. Below her waist there was nothing left, a deflated balloon cast off towards the center of the room.

The ebony horror toddled to the examination table. It was gaining flesh exponentially. When it began its banquet, it rang of abomination.

Watching the creature bob its head, she wondered idly at Larry's replacement.

She had a feeling she'd just met hers.

The morgue was cold, fading towards freezing. Catching a glimpse of her reflection in the stainless steel, she was a crimson-spattered thing, sundered and vital and above all gorgeous amidst the wreckage.

She couldn't look away.

Not even when, above her hip, the letters began to form.

# THRENODY - JO QUENELL

The dead kid's dads lived far from her apartment, in one of the city's "safe" neighborhoods. She arrived early and waited in her beater, hating the heat and her long-sleeved turtleneck. To pass the time she played the piano track on her phone and practiced singing softly. Only a day until the funeral and the words were still tangled in her head.

Before leaving she pulled mace from her glove box and tucked it into her purse. Insensitive, maybe. But necessary, given the reality of everything.

It wasn't any cooler outside the car and she thanked the shade of the three-story house. It took him several minutes to answer once she'd rang the bell and texted her arrival. A part of her hoped he'd never come.

The door opened. Goddamn. No going back.

"Lydia?" asked a somber-faced man. Despite the

house and the neighborhood, he looked like he'd slept in a ditch.

"That's me," she said, offering a smile and feeling wrong about it.

He offered her a limp handshake, and when she looked into his eyes she saw nothing. An unbearable moment passed before he invited her in.

"Excuse the mess," he said, leading her first through a kitchen, then a living room. For all the funerals she had performed at, Lydia had never been invited to a home of the mourning. God, it was bleak. Conciliatory gifts and prepared meals seemed to cover every table and counter- -well-intentioned reminders of loss.

He led her up a flight of stairs, then down a hall. "Thank you for your flexibility," he said, stopping before a door and digging a keychain from his pocket. "I apologize for leaving this to such short notice. "I guess I..." he paused, sighing. "There's been so much to do with no time. I'm behind on everything."

"I completely understand," she said. "I've been listening to the track and practicing alone."

"We both know that's not the same," he said, opening the door.

She'd spent time in studios, back when she thought she could use her gifts to escape. None were as nice as the one he'd built in his own home. He walked over to a Steinway and lifted its fallboard, then gently pressed his fingers against its keys. A mournful melody echoed through the small space. He turned to Lydia, glancing at her like he'd forgotten she was there, then motioned to the duet bench.

"Please, sit."

Lydia nodded and occupied the spot next to him. The familiar stench of old whiskey wafted off of him as he shuffled sheet music, finding the right number. He pressed down on the ivory and began a sad progression on a minor scale. Lydia had heard the original plenty of times in the past week; it was a common number on playlists of popular ceremony songs. But he had warped it into something haunting and heartbreaking. She closed her eyes, listening to the notes fall. At her cue, she began to sing.

The first sour note fell before the second verse began. Others followed, breaking both the song's sullen melody and her ability to focus. She fumbled a line and paused, playing catch-up in her head.

He punched down on the keys, emitting an ear-splitting crash. "Goddamnit, it's not hard."

Lydia's words escaped her. The tension newly filling the rooms was enough to push her off of the bench and out the door. Instead she picked at a torn cuticle at her left thumb and awaited the moment to pass.

"It's not you," he said after a suffocating pause. He didn't make eye contact. "You're good. The moment I heard your recordings, I knew you were the one for this. The problem's me. It's..." he sighed out of either frustration or resignation. "It's not even a hard piece. I just can't make it work."

"We don't need to do this if you can't," Lydia said. She tried padding her voice with comfort, hoping for an excuse to leave.

He shook his head. "No. I need this. I need to get this right." He placed his fingers back on the keys.

"Let's take it from the top."

He poured them each a drink after the fourth failed attempt. They sat in the living room, the silence broken only by the hum of the central air system. She'd tried and failed to make herself comfortable on the corner of a leather sofa while he sank into a recliner across from her. The whiskey loosened him, flattening the tension in his shoulders.

"Your album is good," he said, talking if only to break the silence. "I was surprised to see you giving it away for free. And honestly, to see you doing these kind of gigs."

"Lots of talent in this city," she said. "But only so many chances."

"I hear that." He toasted his empty tumbler before filling it with a second, stiffer pour. "But that's part of the fun, isn't it? Chasing those chances, fueled by that passion? That's why we started, right?"

"It's a lot of fun before the rent's due," she said. She sipped her drink. It burnt going down.

"You'll remember these moments as the good ones." He smiled, and for the first time that day he seemed a bit less deflated. "I remember those first tours sleeping on stranger's floors. Putting every dime into the gas tank. Living that dream, chasing success? It made me feel invincible when I had the most to lose."

"Looks like you reached the finish line," Lydia said, glancing around the exquisitely furnished room.

"The attorney husband has more to thank for that than me," he said. "And once we adopted, that was it. I don't think the dream died for me, as much as it morphed. Kids do that to you. You have any?"

She quickly shook her head and downed the rest of her drink, dreading where the conversation would turn.

"Sorry, rude question." He walked over to her, holding the whiskey decanter, and topped her drink despite her protests. His cheeks had grown rosy under their coarse layer of stubble. The alcohol gave him a sense of liveliness he'd lacked prior. She doubted he'd be letting her leave any time soon. She was a welcome distraction from a brutal reality.

"Let me show you something special," he said, walking to an entertainment center. He pilfered through a pile of burnt DVD discs stacked upside down and selected one. After wiping its underside on his shirt, he slid it into the drive of a fancy Blu Ray player. This time he sat on the couch, close to Lydia. He picked a remote off the coffee table in front of them, scrolling through a generic menu on his TV screen before pressing play.

A piano sat center screen, in what looked to be a reception hall of some sort. Rows of attendants filled the room—families dressed formally, parents whispering stern reminders to young children who'd sat too long. Tacky Christmas decorations livened the walls, and a woman in a festive sweater and a Santa hat announced the next performer. A young boy walked from a right-side entrance, wearing a dress suit too businesslike for a child.

He must have been ten years younger than in the photo all the papers used. For a painful moment, Lydia struggled to breathe.

"He was eight here," he said next to her. "Only playing for two years. Already ahead of the curve."

"It must have helped having you to teach him," she said.

"He was always around music, starting at day one. Ran through the family."

She thought about her sisters. Their familial songs. Fuck. Guilt squeezed her stomach.

The boy onscreen scooted forward on the duet bench until his feet reached the pedals. Fingers on the keys, he began playing.

Not even a minute into the song and the front door opened.

An olive-skinned man with rings under his eyes carried vibrant floral arrangements in his arms, which he sat on the tiles of the entryway. He looked to his husband with a sour look. "Matt? What's going on?"

The father ignored the question, his eyes glued to the screen. His husband turned to her. "Who are you?"

Lydia's face burnt hot with anxiety and whiskey. She stammered out her name.

"She's the singer," the man beside her said, still watching the recital from another life. "We were practicing the song."

His partner scoffed. "Practicing." He picked up the bouquets and walked to the kitchen with an agitated stride. He called from the kitchen, his voice an icepick.

"I've been running errands all damn day and you couldn't even put the food away."

Lydia grabbed her purse from the foot of the couch. "I should go," she said. "I'll practice the song more tonight. I'll be ready tomorrow." She stood and started for the front door.

He sighed, hitting the stop button on the remote. His dead son disappeared, replaced by a black screen. "I just wanted a break," he said.

She was unsure if he said it to her, or anyone in particular. She didn't stay to find out. The yelling started once she shut the front door behind her.

She threw her purse onto the passenger side floor and slumped in her driver's seat, pressing her forehead against the steering wheel. She shut her eyes. The urge to scream or sob was greater than her ability to do either. Instead she sat up, started her car, and sped out of the subdivision, freeing herself from the gated neighborhood and heading back to the city she knew.

She needed another drink.

Then she needed to see her sisters.

The late afternoon heat had peaked, and the beachfront should have been packed. The shores remained secluded. The caution tape had been taken down but nothing had returned to normal. Lydia tucked the fifth she had bought at the liquor store into her purse and stepped out of her car, walking onto the empty shore. The shoreline crept closer to her, the water nearly submerging her feet, greeting her. The smell of the salty brine brought her back to her childhood. It had been months since she'd last visited, and she wondered if all this was punishment. She'd broken a promise, and so had they.

She walked until the rocks on the shore gave away to fine sand, then sat facing the water. She pulled off her boots and buried her feet in the sand, then pulled the fifth from her purse and uncapped it. It was rubbing alcohol compared to the smooth shit earlier, burning like a motherfucker. Lydia held her breath until she was sure it would stay down.

The tide pulled even closer, reaching her ankles. They knew she was here.

Enough time passed that the sun began its westward dip into the horizon. The heat lingered and Lydia rolled her sleeves up, not worried about anybody seeing her. She took occasional pulls off the fifth, regretting each sip.

"I don't know where we go from here," she said finally, staring towards the water. "I'm just really disappointed."

She knew they heard, yet none of them responded. Stubbornness, most likely. *Or maybe shame,* she hoped. Maybe they realized their fortune, graced only by the skepticism of the modern world. The city wrote it off as an accident—a fatal mix of alcohol and youthful confidence. They even rationalized the wild claims from the kid's friends. It simply wasn't possible. Nobody had been singing. The only thing pulling him into the water was the tide.

They were lucky this time. But someone's kid was still dead.

She drank from her bottle. It hurt less going down, but with its burn blossomed rage.

"I met his parents. I saw what this did to them. It's not just his life that's over. Others are suffering."

And still they said nothing. Something inside her snapped. "I can't protect you if you do this shit!" She stood, the effects of the whiskey causing her to stumble. Grabbing her purse and shoes, she started back in the direction she'd come from. The tide stopped moving-- the ocean itself stilled, neither creeping forward or pushing away. Whether or not they regretted their actions, they understood the reality of the moment. They awaited her move.

*Don't bend. Don't show them weakness.*

But she slowed, then stopped. Her anger cratered, broken by the sobering fact before her. And for the first time since seeing the kid's face on the news and tracing the webs of his fate to them, a proper sob escaped her throat.

She knew there was no coming back from this.

The tide pulled closer to her, cautiously creeping along the sand until it submerged her feet. Lydia's knees buckled. She slumped into the briny pool forming below, her whole body deflating. The water soaked her jeans, and with the chilling sensation came a flood of memories. She hadn't stepped into its depths since leaving all those years ago. Her mind floundered in thoughts she'd rather forget. She tried focusing on the present, on the life she'd created for herself since then. It wasn't much, but it was something better.

From the depth of the waters rose a symphony of voices, singing a familiar haunting song. Each memorized word brought with it old sensations. She tasted copper in the back of her throat, and for the first time in years, she yearned for the feel of meat against her molars. Invisible tendrils wrapped around her arm and gently tugged, urging her to join them. Pleading for her to return.

Part of her wanted nothing more than to revert to the old ways. To sing that song once more.

Instead, she stayed on her knees. She clenched her teeth, keeping the words and melody from slipping from her mouth. She leveled the old yearning for the hunt by picturing the damage she could cause. She focused on the kid's face. Drowned out her sister's melodies by humming the song he'd played at his recital.

She stayed still until the singing ended and the tide retreated, leaving her in sand and silence. Without looking to the water, Lydia said a quiet goodbye and left the shore for good.

Lydia woke up on her floor, feeling like termites had gnawed away sections of her brain. Blinding light penetrated through her apartment windows, turning the small studio into a hotbox. The contents of her purse were spilled across the hardwoods around her, and she'd forgotten to close the front door on her way in. It was a

miracle none of her sketchy neighbors had invited themselves in.

She didn't remember much after leaving the beach.
After killing the fifth she'd bought a six pack, then sat
drinking in her car, fighting off the lingering urges to
return to her family. At some point she'd blacked out. It
was nothing short of a miracle that she made it home
alive.

Though judging by her current state, she may as well
be on her deathbed.

The twenty feet from her current spot to the toilet
may as well have been a mile, and it was luck alone that
she made it. Stomach knotted, she leaned over the bowl
and let loose. The bile came first, scalding the back of
her throat. She waited for the unforgiving sting of
alcohol to follow.

Instead cold, murky water hit the porcelain beneath
her. It sprayed out of her like some cheap horror movie
gag, filling up the bowl. Saline burnt her nostrils as it
streamed out of her nose. Flecks of grit and sand sliced
the lining of her throat, giving the water a tinge of red.
She couldn't even fight for breath. The toilet bowl
overflowed.

Something slimy and thick rose, lodging in her wind-
pipe and stopping the flow. Lydia's panic spiked as
dammed water continued to fill her throat. A slippery,
viscous flap tickled the back of her mouth, wagging like a
second tongue as she choked. Lydia stuck fingers into her
mouth, pinching at the flap and pulling. It lurched
forward a mere inch before tearing in her grasp. She tried
again, searching for precision despite the fear of drown-

ing. She grasped the flap again and pulled gently, easing a long, brown rope of seaweed out of her mouth. It fell from her grasp, splatting against worn linoleum. A final burst of backed up water sprayed out of her. Lydia collapsed, coughing, her throat shredded. It felt like she had expelled her entire past, killing a part of herself with it. And it took what felt like years before she could move again.

She turned the shower to hot and let it run until the bathroom filled with steam. She squatted on the floor of the tub, letting burning water rain down on her until the skin on her back and neck was beet red. She ran her hands across her thighs and arms, feeling the shameful patches she'd tried in vain to hide with sleeves and long dresses. She considered getting a knife and descaling herself until she leaked gore, then taking a needle and thread to the gills splitting each side of her neck. At the end of it all she'd look like some Frankenstein's monster covered in scars and stitches, yet finally free.

But she thought of all the ways it could go bad. Maybe shock or loss of blood would be too much. In a week her super would kick open her door after a neighbor complained about the stench, only to find her naked and bloated with rot. What would they think at the sight of the scales she couldn't scrape free, or a weeping gill half-shut by home surgery? Could someone connect her existence to the tall stories from the kid's bewildered friends?

She couldn't let that happen. Turning away from her sisters felt like enough of a betrayal. She wouldn't be the reason they were found.

She spent the morning packing, breaking only to fight the hangover bouts. She decided she'd take only what could fit in the back of her car. The rest the super could dump behind the building for the homeless to filter through. She had no set plan. Didn't know how much gas she could get with the meager contents of her checking account. The deposit from the kid's fathers would help. Pangs of guilt filled Lydia at the thought of leaving without giving the performance they'd paid for. But she didn't think it was possible to look them in the eyes again, given everything. After loading up the things she deemed important, Lydia placed the key to her apartment on the floor of the entryway. She left the door open and didn't look back.

She had never been further than a mile out of the city before. Didn't know which exit would take her where. As Lydia drove aimlessly it became more apparent that she had no working plan, had little hope of getting far before running out of resources. She circled around, second guessing, cursing herself for wasting needed gas. An address ran through her mind, fueled by guilt pushing her to make things right before moving on. She tried shaking the thought free, but instead found herself turning back around, getting closer each time. She'd turned off her phone to avoid their calls, as a way to resist this very thing. There was no point in going--she was late already, an hour past the start time. And she wouldn't be able to sing, not after a morning of vomiting sea water and brine. Her voice was little more than a ragged croak.

Maybe she needed to confess--give them the truth, and herself a clean conscience.

Maybe she wasn't ready to run.

Cars packed the lot of the reception hall, so Lydia parked on a side street. The sight of him standing on the front lawn filled her guts with ice. What moments before seemed inevitable now felt impossible. He'd cleaned up since the day before—hair parted, stubble shaved off. His suit easily cost more than her steep rent. The despair and defeat in his shoulders was now replaced by tension and rage. He pressed a phone against his ear and yelled into the mouthpiece. He pinched a cigarette between the fingers of his free hand and sucked angrily at its filter in between breaths. Lydia wondered how many angry messages he had left in her voicemail. He didn't even seem like the same sad man she'd sat next to on the piano bench. The sight of him made her feet heavier than concrete blocks.

*What the fuck am I doing here?* she thought.

The door of the reception hall opened. The man's husband walked out, also dressed sharply. He'd aged years within a day. He approached his partner, each step heavy with exhaustion. With grace, he took the phone from his partner and killed the call.

The man blew up, screaming, pointing at his spouse with fingers clutching the cigarette. His partner remained neutral. Their roles had reversed from the day before—one's hurt fueled anger, while the other simply tried to survive. Nothing Lydia could do or say would take their hurt away. She couldn't come clean. Not here. Not today.

One day her sisters would slip up. One day they'd be

found out. When that day came, she'd be long gone, living a different life somewhere landlocked.

The couple remained out front, one screaming, the other calmly taking it. Attendees gathered out by the doors, watching the conflict, too timid to intervene. Eventually he ran out of angry words and curses, and as his rage diminished, the grief returned. He slumped into his partner's arms, sobbing. The two men held each other tight. In time mourners moved away from the door and toward the broken men, embracing them. Slowly, they led the men off of the lawn and back into the reception hall. They filtered inside, leaving Lydia alone and watching from afar.

Once the last one entered, Lydia started her car and drove away.

# THE QUEEN OF THE SELECT - KATY MICHELLE QUINN

**M**erlot,

You are cordially invited to this season's upcoming Soiree of the Select. Your display at last season's event caught our notice, and your place as a fellow arbiter of taste will be reviewed at the upcoming gathering on the 7$^{th}$ of August.

As always, please dress appropriately for an event of such sophistication. Per pandemic regulations, a release must be signed by all in attendance who are not properly masked. A robe will be loaned to you for the duration of the festivities. Your utmost candor is requisite and appreciated, and the aforementioned consequences will be upheld should that be breached.

We expect your presence to be sweet as our finest vintage.

Sincerely,

The Vintner's Estate

The letter hadn't come through the mail. These matters required more discretion than the United States Postal Service could provide. As instructed during the Vintner's last gathering, Steven had found the wine red envelope taped to the bottom of a public bench two blocks up the hill from the Capitol Hill Police Station. He had just gotten off duty, and the stroll had seemed unsuspicious despite his blue uniform and lack of the mandatory face covering. With the COVID crisis still gripping the city tight, there were few onlookers to see the policeman crouch to search the underside of the paint-tagged bench. He'd passed one other walker on his way, a wraith of a woman geared with torn black jeans and a dirty hoodie emblazoned with a logo that looked like gnarled roots. The bandana she'd tied around her face would've been a red flag to him had they not been in the midst of a pandemic. He'd taken down plenty like her, though not all so pretty.

The smell of stale smoke wafts past him as he passes. He turns to cross-examine her ass, spits on the ground when her gait gives her away as a ladyboy. Gives *him* away, should say. Steven had lived here long enough to remember a time when they were too afraid to be seen in the daylight, and often he missed the better days.

As if she could hear his thoughts, she had turned to hiss through her bandana before slinking down an alley toward Cal Anderson.

Once he'd unstuck the envelope from the bench, he'd hid it beneath his shirt for the walk back to his squad car. He'd over-practiced the story that it was an anniversary card for his wife, filled it with details that were believable but vague, should anyone on the force ask. But better to skip the suspicion. He'd found that hiding well is the best defense against being uncovered for what you were. Times like these, there were enough eyes on him as it was. To live in a state as red as his hidden envelope, maybe that was the answer. No more side stepping the threat in the name of bureaucracy. He'd once again be able to grab the bull by the horns and beat it.

The thought puts him in a better mood, along with the prospect of what's to come. He hums something simple as he crouches into his car and jets away from the station.

Brandy wakes up in the Castle. This is the fourth morning rising to the endless flickering that licks the walls of the stone-splattered room she sleeps in, splayed bellylong on the hard floor like a reclining panther. The women around her repose, curled up on the floor, sleeping ceiling-hung like bats, all queens of their own kingdoms.

The Castle is the first place Brandy had ever been where everyone was like her. Women born a way the majority weren't. Women who were told, maybe believed, they weren't women at all. Brandy had been there, for too long. She was into adulthood before she read the leaves that fell from her tree of life too soon. A wet message that spoke of a better life, one apart from boyhood. She'd ran away from what she had been and never looked back, toward a difficult life, but one that was worth living.

The resting women around her knew this story in their own way. They had conquered adversity to become the royalty they always were. Bodies were revered when the curtains closed, and lovers could suck their secret without the shame of it. It's how Brandy had gotten by, likely how many of the rest had, too. You take the opportunities you're given when so few are presented.

She had been working when she was taken to the Castle. Her last memory of the outside is the sweatfunk of an older john's dick as she licked it like a lolly. A memory she'd be fine forgetting. She'd never taken to the work like some did. She'd never considered herself truly, honestly sexy.

Until she was taken here.

In the Castle, where she is worshipped like a royal. She is queen here, days spent reclining naked in swathes of silk, her sex swinging freely like succulent fruit. No need to tuck it away anymore. Here, she is adored for precisely what she is. She is lavished and brought gifts of fruit and drink, cocktails of unknown origin containing a liquor of bliss.

She salivates now at the thought of their sweetness.

As if she had been heard, steps echo down the staircase that leads to her chambers. The clack of leather soles against something like stone. The sound of sustenance. Brandy can't tell if it's her hunger or the length of the staircase, but the steps stretch on forever. It feels like hours before the shape of one of the Maidmen emerges. This one is white, his unshirted torso reflecting the flickering lamplight. He holds a domed platter of gold in his sturdy hands. Brandy wishes he would hold her. Many men had held her since she came to the Castle, but this one is new. His golden hair slides down his skull, and his dark eyes look like dirt-dug holes she'd happily lie down in. She wants him almost as much as she wants what's on the platter. Almost.

S teven hates this part, the theater of it. He'd much prefer a double-draught of the good stuff without all the pinky-lifting and punplay. He stands back to the polished oak wall in a rented tux, second Old Fashioned down to the bitters, waiting for the social downpour to let up. Disenchanted as he is, though, he hopes his inaptitude for enculturation doesn't count against him. Sure, he only cares about what's in the cellar, but if he has to wade through upper-crust cock-gobblers to get there, so be it.

In the middle of the ballroom, a tall, thin man in a red silk smoking jacket flits through the smattering of attendees like it's sport. The man spots Steven, tying up the loose ends of the current conversation before he walks over.

"Mr. Vintner," Steven says, nodding his greetings.

"Merlot!" the man pulls him into the awkward embrace of the alabaster elite. "So glad you could make it."

"Wouldn't miss it for the world."

His charm goes stale before the words wear off. The

Vintner feels it, too. The tall man runs a skeletal hands down Steven's back, causing the stiff man to shiver inadvertently.

"It's okay," he says into Steven's ear. "Loosen up. We're here to have fun."

Steven lets a shaky breath blow and shimmies his shoulders, an open ploy to remove the man's hand from his back.

"Of course, sir."

"Believe it or not, I wasn't always the butterfly you see before you. I've spent my time plastered to posh walls."

Steven nods.

"You're here because you belong here," the Vintner tells him. "Give us another display tonight, and your membership is guaranteed."

"Yes, sir. Thank you, sir."

The Vintner downs his snifter and clears his throat.

"In the meantime, why don't you chat up some folks?" he says, eyes sifting for the next social interaction. "You might even make a friend."

"Of course, sir," Steven says, watching the man wash into the crowd.

His words meet empty air.

He slams the rest of his drink and shudders off the nerves. He knows why he's here. He more than makes up for his lack of social prowess with what he does during the night's festivities. A display, indeed. He'll show them a fucking *spectacle*.

B randy hates it when the Tall Man comes down the stairs. He interrupts her court like an unwanted jester, ballying about as if it is he who owns the place, the red velvet of his jacket hinting at the low lamplight. He always wears a mask, they all do, besides the Maidmen. White, featureless things likely purchased bulk from a party supply company. Effective, though, in hiding the faces of her enemies. It becomes much harder to be angry at the man whose face you cannot see.

Brandy feels herself start to fume. How dare he prance in here without permission, poisoning the sanctity of her space. The others hang silently, as they always do. Why is it up to her to speak, again?

"Get out," she says, her tone royal. "I do not want you here."

The man chuckles, his laugh as cavernous as the Castle.

"But my queen," he mocks, "I've brought you the finest vintage."

He pulls a vial from the chest pocket of his coat, it's wine-red fluid sloshing silently inside. The man never stops closing in on her, his movements as careful and endless as a cat. Brandy wants to move, but she can't. It's as if she were chained in place, absurd as that seems. Who would dare take the Queen prisoner?

"I do not want your gifts."

The Tall Man snaps fingers, and the two Maidmen flanking him fall back. He steps closer to her, and in a moment of brashness grabs her chin in his lanky fingers.

"Guards!" Brandy gasps, but no one responds.

The Tall Man laughs.

"You're aging well, darling," he tells her. He inhales deeply, his nostrils centimeters from skin. "That sweetness, that must, it's the best sign of decay. It means you're starting to ferment."

He licks her from chin to cheek. "Mmm, you will be some of the finest I've produced. Not like the others."

The tall man releases her and begins to walk the line of women beside her.

"They're nice enough to the uninitiated, but a true connoisseur will know. They've grown stale, lost their flavor, their feel."

He prods at one of the women, and she does nothing. He touches her again, lingering this time.

"Although," he says, breathy, "even the cheapest wine is meant to be drunk."

He latches onto her like a carrion bird, his mouth against hers.

Something is wrong here. Why is the woman motionless? Why isn't she fighting, running away from this ravisher. Brandy makes to stop him only to feel something biting at her wrists. She looks up and sees a metal snake hanging from the ceiling above her. The stonework of the Castle seems dirtier than before, gray smeared with all shades of dark.

"Where am I?"

She pulls against the chains, but they are rooted too deep in the dungeon walls.

"What the FUCK?!"

Brandy vomits down her naked front. Her vision clears to show the skinny socialite coddling a corpse, his living lips locked onto broken bits of flesh and coagulated globules of blood. The Tall Man releases his lover of the moment and approaches her, retrieving the vial from his pocket. His mouth drips with gore as if he was a lion that had just eaten.

"Get away get away getaway from me!" Brandy screams.

She struggles away from the tall man's approach, but the chains hold her closely. He snaps in the air before pulling a syringe from the same pocket the vial had come from. Brandy feels the strong grip of the Maidmen as they restrain her, giving the tall man a moment to slip the needle into the vein of her arm.

"No no no no no no no no."

"Drink up, darling," the man says. "The finest vintage."

For only a moment, as reality releases its hold on her, she recognizes the features of the dead body hanging next to her.

"Misty," she slurs, before her friend disappears.

The jazz trio that occupied one corner of the ballroom stop playing without announcement. Steven looks over in time to see the Vintner mounting the six-inch stage they're standing on, drink dangling from a willowy grip. He graciously accepts a proffered microphone from the trio's lead blower.

"Thank you," his first amplified words, gaze still regarding the brassman as if he was a brimming cocktail glass.

On cue, everyone claps.

Steven joins the applause despite the fact that all this theater makes him sick enough to throw up all six-and-a-half Old Fashioneds. But he's a man made to stomach the sour. If he wasn't, he wouldn't be here. The Soiree was not a place for the gimp-gutted.

His vision blurs to the taste of barrel-aged bourbon and bitters. As the Vintner begins his two-faced tirade, sound becomes cumulus. A vast, floating whole just out of Steven's reach. He settles back against the wall, hoping the structure will shake off the feeling of falling into empty space.

This is what happens when it awakens. Steven calls it the Beast, a fact he would never admit outside the confines of his inner dialogue. Steven's as sane as a man can get, but even he struggles to define what exactly the Beast is. Not a separate personality, nothing so lavish as that. More like moving on auto-pilot, but that times ten. As if the off-drippings of rage left unexpressed collect at the bottom of his stomach and give birth to something greater than their sum. A monster erupting from a puddle of poison.

Steven had known The Beast since birth. As a child, the increasing incidents of its release led his parents to drag him across the country to the West Coast just to get away from the fear in everyone's eyes. That experience, combined with the competing appetites of puberty, taught him to drown out its roar with whatever means he could. First it was isolation, midnight movings after his parents slept, then it was cars, women, and whiskey, preferably at the same time. All the while, fangs prover-bially growing from his canines.

The Beast had laid dormant for almost a decade, a few overblown bar brawls notwithstanding, but when he had begrudgingly accepted the invite of a former cop friend to last season's soiree, he had rediscovered his teeth. It led to this, after all. He had never known that there were others that were, in their own way, like him. He was chief predator among them, though. Even the patrons of this sinister party regarded him with care, kept their distance so as not to get drawn into the under-tow. Already Merlot was something of a name.

Or it would be, if he doesn't fuck up this time.

The blur remains, blocking out everything except the thudding of the Beast's claws against his inside. It wants out, and he'll let it, but only when the time is right. Releasing it too early would only end in disaster. One more whiskey should do the trick.

As he heads to the back bar, though, he's interrupted.

"Mr. Merlot," the mic squeals.

Steven stops in his tracks, his brain already trained to the codename. He turns to see the Vintner waving him to the stage. The upscale audience watches him patiently.

*All I wanted was one more fucking drink.*

Steven smiles a slit and walks through the parted crowd. He doesn't want to be shown, to be known, but how can he say no under the circumstance? He steps onto the stage and the Vintner wraps him in an arm as long as a tentacle.

"Our newest hopeful," the tall man enunciates.

To Steven, his words sound miles away. He's already losing his connection to the man he daywalks as. The Beast is beginning to bare its fangs, thirsty at the thought of blood to come. Steven wipes slobber from his mouth with the sleeve of his rented suit. He can feel his weapon thumping against his zipper. He gnashes his teeth, the feeling of flesh a phantom in his mouth.

"A few words, Merlot? Before we begin."

The Vintner holds the mic in front of Steven's face.

Steven can hear his breath echo in the eaves of the ballroom.

"I'll try to leave some for everyone else," he says.

Chuckles erupt around the room.

The Vintner laughs and takes the mic for a final phrase.

"Friends, colleagues. Now is the time for the tasting."

The crowd bubbles over like a bad bottle of wine. The Maidmen materialize around the ballroom as if from the wooden walls themselves, arms full of silk the shade of Sauvignon. The two on the stage approach the Vintner and Steven, who shudders at the sudden pres-ence behind him. It's a moment before he has the mind to stand like a man at the tailor's in preparation. The strong hands of the shirtless man behind him feel for his shoulders, then pull at the lapel of his blazer until it gives way and slides free. Immediately, another set of hands loosens and removes his tie, begins undoing his buttons. Half-undressed, Steven looks the part of the beast. His concrete chest sprouts a field of dark hair that bursts from his shirt like water from a dam. As the Maidmen begin to undo his trousers, the button pops with anticipation, and his steel-stiff cock presses against his briefs like it's spring-loaded. For a second Steven is left nearly naked in the light of the stage, his bear-like body provoking the onlookers until the Maidmen slip the silk robe over his shoulders. He pulls the hood up, becoming instantly the member of a blood cult he is.

A sea of black ties turns to deep red silk as the Maidmen dress the rest for the final event. Steven can't tell one asshole from another under their cavernous hoods. He turns to the Vintner, now identically adorned, who nods. The Maidmen collect and lead the two down a dark hallway. The congregation follows, eager for a taste of heaven.

**B**randy surveys her kingdom. She wraps her wrists in chains that are rosy gold in her eyes. The Royal Feast is minutes away, and she must look her absolute best. Her forearms ooze the deepest rouge, and with a finger she dips and decorates her lips, the apples of her cheeks. Just to give them a little bit of life.

She knows the feast approaches because of the thundering heavens. Above the Castle, there has been a sound like slowly stampeding horses for hours. In her dreams, a goddess had told her this would signify a celebration.

*How long have I been here?*

The drugbuzz brushes the thought away like one of the many bloated flies floating through the Throneroom. They gather like guests of the Feast, eagerly awaiting the sweetmeat to come. Drawn as if to rot.

*Why am I wet?*

Another fly swatted. The thundering stops for a minute, and the drone of a voice Brandy recognizes echoes off the walls. She shivers at the thought of the Tall Man. If she had her way, he would not be in attendance.

*Earth to Brandy, Misty is dead. They're all dead, and you're next. Wake up, they're coming.*

The thundering above resumes, drowning out all the unpleasantry. It gets louder, closer somehow, until Brandy can hear it reverberating down the stairs that lead to the Throneroom. The gallop of fine leather oxfords against hard stone steps. She knows the sound. That sound means rich. That sound means royalty.

Suitors. They must be. People coming to compete for her love, for the chance to sit beside her. Brandy reclines, refreshes the red on her face, and waits wordlessly like the queen she is.

Steven hears the coughs, the retching behind him without acknowledgement. Second Soiree in, he's already a seasoned pro. A thick splat behind tells him than an initiate has lost their stomach. It smells especially acidic, the Noir they were drinking evident in the air. Steven can feel rivulets of the stuff lick against his exposed soles, but he keeps moving. Not that he could stop. The Beast has smelled his prey.

"Drat," comes the Vintner's voices just aft. "Jerome,

can you help our guest to the wellness room? Please and thank you?"

Steven doesn't have to see to know that one of the shirtless Maidmen is now helping another robe back up the stairs. The crowd stutters around the interruption like hesitant water.

"Watch your step, please," the Vintner impares. He snaps. "Clean this up." Then, directed at the general area, "Please keep in mind that our events are not for everyone. Practice discretion in who you bring with you."

Steven feels a bony hand on his shoulder. The Vintner, maybe seeking comfort, assurance that he is not the only one who takes pleasure in this. There's something so lonely in sharing your passions with another only to have them vomit at your feet.

But he won't find comfort here. No one will. Steven, and the whirlwind inside him, is a tool of discomfort. Destruction.

He steps into the glow concluding the long staircase down. The rest of the robes backfill the room, tense as drawn bows.

His first glance is a deep drink of her beauty. This event's queen hangs by her wrists from chains looped through grommets in the ceiling. Her posture, a product of the drugs, is almost lackadaisical, her skeleton collapsing without the support of sleeping tendons. She'll be fully limp soon enough, a succulent cut of meat curing in the cold basement air.

The queen, like the others, is the sort of woman Steven would never be seen with aboveground. The kind he would put in their place to prove the kind of man he is. The kind he'd faggot-fought behind a bar on more than one occasion, the kind that barely fought back, limp wrists whacking uselessly at his bulk. But the Beast has appetites. The mouthfeel, the taste of halfsoft cock in his mouth. So sweet you could almost bite it off clean. The skinny curve of slight but beautiful hips in his hands, so delicate you could crush them into dust. As if in response, the queen's sex throbs near imperceptively, a minute awakening.

Unlike the others, she still breathes. The bodies around her resist their bonds with the gravitational weight of the dead, their flesh flocked with flies. These are for the initiates, the posers, Steven thinks. Those weak ones who want a taste of decay without bringing it about themselves. But he knows there's nothing like corpse you make yourself. This is what had caught the Vintner's eye at the last event. While most newcomers would fret about the bodies like anxious children before choosing one, always one without life, Steven made his choice as soon as he heard the softly choking breath. Without a word, he had strolled forward, confident, and sunk his teeth into the flesh of her neck, inserting himself into her with a killing thrust. The sound she made next he had never heard anything like. An orgasm while the life leaves you must be quite confusing. At just the thought, Steven hardens against the surprise he has strapped to his dick.

The Vintner separates from the crowd of crimson, removing his hood so as to regain authority.

"Welcome to my cellar," he tells them, arms wide. "Everything you see is here for your pleasure. You may bite, chew, or fuck any flesh at your discretion. We encourage you to try as much as you can."

The Vintner steps over a body slumped on the floor and crouches next to one leaning against the wall. This corpse is older, where the Vintner's tastes lean, Steven knows, and her flesh has long begun to sag. Her dark skin is parched by decay, wrinkles decorating what in life was smooth as silk. Her small breasts hang low, as if melting down her torso, and her twiggy limbs have the look of chicken wings left out for the night, skin ripped, bones exposed, flies feeding. But her face is the jewel. Limp lips slide towards the hem of her skull, and open eyelids candle-wax down, letting what's left of her vitreous humor ooze out of irises stretched wider than a porn-star's asshole.

The Vintner gathers a bit of the goop on the tip of a finger before slurping it up with savor.

The tall man groans with pleasure as he stands back up.

"The three-month Puerto Rican is especially succulent," he tells the crowd. "Now, please! Feast!"

Duties as host completed, the Vintner lets his robe slip off him, revealing a geriatric frame in black briefs and vultures down to the corpse for another mouthful.

The crimson crowd mutters uncertainly, a few venturing forward to inspect the vintage. Posers, all. Steven knew it. He'll show them. He shrugs off his silk, baring the Beast's svelte, muscular form. His life outside is dedicated to this, to keeping his temple tuned. It's his only religion, striving for the certainty that he will never be bested in body. His pale skin bulges, sinew moving over his skeleton like a pit of snakes. He strides out from the crowd, an obvious leader, and makes his way towards the queen who clings to life by the tiniest of threads.

Her eyes flutter open, though they seem to see things that aren't there. He hopes she sees him, he hopes she fears what's to come. But Steven's steps studder as memory dresses her frame in tattered black. Those fluttery eyes like knives poking over a bandana. This is the girl, the one he had passed the day he got the invite. The one who had given him daggers without even knowing his name. She had been beautiful then, though he would never have admitted it by light, but she's even more beautiful now. Hung from chains, her body curves deliciously, like fresh meat on a spit. Steven steps in to take a taste.

No one asks Brandy for an audience with her, but she brushes off the small insult, deigning instead to drink the sweet liquid proffered to her lips. Her rouge smears the small glass, red painted onto darker red.

The size of the crowd is substantial, much larger than those she'd had in the past, making her think that previous occurrences were practice for tonight. Whatever is happening, this is the big event. She remembers her posture, pulls her spine straight as if drawn by a string (queens aren't supposed to slouch).

They're all dressed in red, cloaks the precise color of the coat the Tall Man typically wore. Hoods drawn, the only way she can tell he's here is how far he grows from the flock. A mother bird amongst its miniatures.

"You may approach," Brandy enunciates.

She is sure her words infused the room with her potence, but the crowd only stirs and murmurs anxiously, unaware she had spoken. Momentarily, the tall man wades through the others towards her. He slips off his hood, exposing his hawkish features. He, more than anyone she had ever seen, has the face of a villain. She *tsk*s under her breath and examines the walls to belay her boredom. She supposes his presence is a necessary evil, he is after all the master of these ceremonies. His say-so sets fire to the festivities. Brandy primes herself for his touch, knowing he couldn't possibly pass by the jewel of the room. It's something she has to suffer before she sees what else is in store. Instead, the tall man takes up with one of the women beside her, a broken-eyed waif of a thing that Brandy had hardly noticed snuck into her court.

*How* dare *he*.

She is the *Queen*. She is the sole symbol of beauty in this court. This is *her* feast, no other's. As if it were possible, she stands taller, looks more disinterested, clings to her displeasure in the hope of sparing her dignity. It seems to be working. One of the crimson horde locks eyes with her. Boyish blues glowing out of a hood, fiber optic. She looks away, a lady after all, but she can feel the holes burning into her skin. The electric moment she had been waiting for. The moment she infects her suitor with untenable desire. His hands might as well already be on her, his fingers gently squeezing her throat as he thrusts.

Brandy coughs the fantasy away. She can't fall so easily. It is up to him to earn her, not the other way around.

*Come here, boy. Come serve your queen.*

She speaks only with eyes.

He hears her, and he approaches.

S teven doesn't usually dress for events, but in this case he has to, barring dismissal from the Select. He had discreetly carried a rented tux from his squad car to the house like the body of a victim. His wife hadn't noticed as he ghosted behind her, busy in the kitchen, to place it in the loosened vent in the utility room. He'd sat there for minutes to the sounds of the sink faucet running at full.

The night of, as planned, she had gone to her sister's, an event he'd escaped by lying about his shift schedule for the week. Duty calls, after all. This gave him time to perfect the pre-game ceremony he had started planning a month before.

Steven wasn't a groomer, but he groomed for this. He wanted everyone to see the Beast for the sophisticated creature it was, not just some bloody ape of a man. He shaved his face and his scrotum, trimmed the bush above his cock and the overgrowth on his chest. When he was done, he could've graced the pages of GQ.

But there was one thing missing, something he had

thought of at the last Soiree, something he had kicked himself for not bringing. The free blade of a Buck knife he had found while running one morning. It was rusty, but not for long. He'd been holding onto to it to rehome in wood, some customized handle he could be proud of. Then the Soiree happened, and his creativity had reawakened.

Stood naked in the mirror, Steven had taken his cock and given it a few strokes to firm it up, grabbed the blade with his free hand. He'd slid it snug between his dickgrip and the flesh before reaching for the zip-ties he had cut to measure.

In the mirror some future soldier of sex, erection crafted from cold steel. It had been a fight to keep the spunk inside.

At this point the Beast has taken over completely, erasure of the man inside. His circuitry floods with raw rage, with pure lust, with gallons of toxic testosterone. He is a machine now, an embodiment of human violence. He seeks only to taste pain, to harvest love out of the throbbing pulp that was another being.

He doesn't scurry away like some of the others, imbibing in their secret shame alone, unseen in one of the myriad chambers the basement holds. Whatever atrocities he will enjoy, he will enjoy right in plain view. Call him an educator in his way.

He begins, like a good predator, with one hard bite to the throat. Leave it alive enough to moan, but not to move. The blood that rivers out is hot and sweet, seasoned with the aftermarket pills she took to remove the boy, to build the body. He's tasted it once before, but this one, this beauty, is transcendent. She tastes of things the world's most expensive spices can't rival. Intricacies that will take years to fully fold into his skull. Something that bites back like capsaicin, something darker than black coffee. A peaty umami the distilleries of Scotland would murder for.

As he drinks it in, the Beast's body relaxes, lost in the savor for a second. But a rattling choke revives him, the Queen's mandatory response to his lover's kiss. He unjaws and pulls back, smiles with winestained teeth as he reads her expression. Whatever they had given her isn't strong enough to block out this level of pain. Vocal cords crushed, her eyes scream for help from the one thing that won't give it to her. Her agony is cut with recognition, both of him and of her expiry. She sees him on the street again, strolling by in his daily blues, badge shining in what little light Seattle offers. He had hoped she would. Their eyes meet with the intimacy of strangers that have seen each other before, wondering whether this is it, this is the next person that will mean something to me, if only for a moment.

And a moment is all it will be. He'll have to hurry.

He wraps one arm around to hold her up and takes her genitals in his other hand. They're smooth and soft, small and round and sticky with sweat. He will taste them soon. Right now he has to focus. He strokes her cock until he sees the confusion of it come up. She doesn't know why, but she is close to cumming. He turns her body around and pulls the band of his briefs down. He doesn't have to get hard because he's hard already, his penis kept stiff and straight by the blade affixed to it.

The Beast kisses the back of her neck, her shoulder blades. He suckles two of his fingers before snailing them down her spine and slipping them into her. Her body goes stiff, he hopes in protest. *Stay alive just a second longer. I'm almost there.* A moment of massaging her hole and she hardens in his hand. *Good girl.* He continues stroking as he spears himself into her rose, cumming as the blood begins to cascade of her ample, round ass. She makes a sound without signifiers, an ululating series of nothings that compose her closing comments. It's a sad sound, one that makes tears spill down his cheeks and mix into the blood. As he thrusts in and out, the blade making a river of her intestines, he releases his own call of confusion. Half beast-man yell, half child's tears, it bounces off the stone walls alongside hers, creating a cacophony of discordant notes hardly distinguishable as human.

After a moment, her cry stops and she slumps into his arms. He continues screaming long enough only to cum once more, his spunk mixing with her sweet blood as he pulls his bladed member out of her beautiful body. He gathers some of the cocktail on his fingertips and tastes it, releasing her finally to hang limply by the wrists, juices running down her chest and legs.

It is only then that he realizes that the room is silent. What few are left have abandoned their own tastings to watch his display. The Vintner approaches, arms outstretched. He pulls him in for an unwanted hug then releases him.

"Absolute magic," he says, his voice trembling, his eyes wet. "Such gorgeous ferocity."

She had cum, she's fairly certain, put it's just a pulse under the pain. Her guts grovel as sharp edges play along her inner surfaces. She's no longer unaware, no longer living in the lie the drugs told her. The effects fled once she was wounded, cascading out of her with the blood he's made her pour. There's no denying who he is now. The cop in him had shown itself once she was lucid, her dreams of fucking dispelled as she was fucked. The unmasked man in blue she had passed with daggers on. She can still hear the sound of his spit hitting the side-walk. And they say she's the pig.

The barbiturate blur leaves her like a guilty walker-by that can't stand to watch the suffering, and she sees the Castle for what it is. Some rich fuck's dirty basement, more torture chamber than sex dungeon. A copse of crimson figures gape at the man who just mutilated her, mouths stuffed with more than they can chew. One escapes up the stairs without heeding the aftercalls.

Brandy's body burns, the network of her nerves elec-tric with the signals being sent to her brain. She chokes on her broken throat, splats something thick onto the stone she can barely stand on. She shudders and mobs as much breath into her body as shock allows.

The cop is not the only familiar face here. The tall man speaking to him (it must be his home it must), she knows him, too. What seems like forever ago, he was a fresh face on her phone, a well-dressed dandy among headless torso after dick pic. His messages were lonely poems praising her beauty, dripping with the desperation of the closeted statesman.

*This,* she tells herself, *is why you never trust a man, no matter how sweet his smile.*

She hangs limp on the chains, wary to give any sign of life. In her experience, they wanted you to react. That's the fun of it. If you dead-dog them, maybe they leave you alone. Maybe you get a chance to run, to fight.

But her fire burns down, and she can't help but fall against her chains. She slips out like a whale into the waves, silently and without notice. After eternity, she surfaces again.

She stands, and her arms float down to her sides. Had someone freed her? Surveying the scene, nothing has changed. The bulky man still smiles menacingly at a crowd of crimson hoods. His mouth is still wet with what used to flow through her.

But there is a difference.

The women around her, the silent women she had seen in her dream, they're back. They're standing, and they're free, the chains that bound them circling their feet like dead snakes. They're awake and breathing, breasts rising with every inhale. They're screaming now, a shrill and harsh sound like a powerdrill on steel. They scream, and she screams with them. They're angry, and she's angry with them.

Despite the cacophony, no one else reacts. The monster-man heaves, his hormones feeding each breath. The crimson onlookers frozen. No reaction. The tallest comes forward, seemingly at Brandy and the others, but actually to the man.

Why does no one hear them?

As if it were possible, the women scream louder, the sound of a storm taking the coast. Brandy looks around her, and the women look back. Misty, the one she knew before, is contorted with pain or anger or both, the animal of her more visible than ever. Her teeth snap together, the sound echoing. It's the signal.

They leap as one. Whether or not their teeth have evolved, whether or not they were really fangs or not, they tear through his flesh like serrated blades, a mob of mouths clamping quick as vipers. Chunks of raw meat fall from his frame, splatting to a stop in puddles of his fluids. As one, they swipe at the chewed-up man, a hundred acrylic tips taking ribbons of skin with them. They fall to the floor, collecting like discarded clothes on a lover's carpet.

The man screams at his hands, examining the pound of flesh his forearm is free of.

Brandy and the women weave together impossibly, a whirlwind of the deceased swirling around the yelling hulk. Their features stretch psychedelically, marbling together until one woman is indistinct from another. The candles that light the walls flicker in the wind of their movement. The crimson cloaks scatter back, the tall man falling and crabbing away from the storm, eyes wide.

The spirits flurry faster, scraping off skin with pointed fingers, splaying off steaks with sharpened teeth. Spinning and spinning faster, what once was a man flecking off one piece after another, skin down to muscle,

muscle down to organs, innards exploding like gore-filled balloons pierced by knives. The force of the swirling spirits sprays macerated flesh in swathes of wet red like a blender left open. The crimson-cloaked attendees receive the brunt of the breeze, faces painted the hue of the silk they wear. A few flee finally, unfrozen by adrenaline. One man licks his lips in a moment of bravery before he vomits on the stone floor.

The spirits whirl so fast it's howling, taking what once was a man down to bone.

At this point, they settle, their figures taking form as if from air, a coven come for retribution. In the center of them, bloody bones rattle to the ground.

It becomes quiet enough to hear the wind outside.

Finally, the tall man breaks the silence.

"What are you?"

The women turn towards him. Brandy speaks, and they speak as one.

"But, Daddy," they hiss. "Don't you remember me?"

Brandy walks down Broadway, black bandana covering her nose and mouth. In other locales, her all-blacks, tattered and tattooed with patches and pins, her ghostly gait and the way it carries her frame across the cement, her skin a shade darker, these are things that would set her apart. That's why she likes it here. On the Hill, she's one of the crowd. She can't walk down the street without seeing a few like her dodging through the thoroughfare, even with the virus keeping most at home.

Today she's making her way to Volunteer Park for a date. They don't come as often this last fistful of months, but she let herself spring for this one. They'd keep masks on for most of it, at least until they see if they connect, and the park is big enough they can distance accordingly.

She's trying not to have a good feeling about this one, but she can't help it. She tells herself it's just for lack of getting laid during the slim days of COVID-19. But her heart flutters as she thinks of the conversations they'd had over the past week on the app. She didn't talk to many people that loved horror like she did, but he was among the few. He'd told her of flicks she'd never heard named, sidestreet cinemas she didn't know existed. He was older, sure, but reasonably so, and in an almost sexy way. His peppered hair popped in contrast to screen after screen of skin. His red velvet jacket was a quirk, that's for sure, but not an unforgivable one. In any case, it spoke of money, which was something she could always use more of. It wouldn't be the first time she'd fucked to get something financial. That's how it was, more often than not, with older men seeking trans companions. The gifts were an unsaid oath of silence common among the closeted elite. She could care less as long as she could pay rent and get something small for herself, an extra ounce of Blue Dream, dinner by delivery, sky's the limit. That's all this will be, she tells herself, another payday. Even so, her lips curved up under the mask, the unforced smile invisible to anyone but her. But maybe. Maybe it could be more.

A girl, after all, can dream.

## SWANMORD - JOANNA KOCH

King Hera slaps the ground and another zoo sutures through the concrete. Her eyes don't open. Her facial flesh puckers. Lids rot closed, slits under dung of swans placed there as a poultice. Healed, her eyes implode. New museums birth atrocity in every flex. Her sword flags. Her codpiece wags. Blooming like candy, king mother Hera births the next exhibit due to populate the bestiary: clove, astringent, and amaranth. Corporeal, she sings a son towards a swan dive. Hayden takes two pills from his stash and confirms sufficient inventory to unmother an existence blooded on protest. With appropriate doses, he'll make it through the night before smashing the whole damn archive.

In a tenor too high to persuade, Hayden serenades Trillious. "I am the DJ, I am what I play." He traverses the room on tip-toes, teetering on invisible high heels. At the foot of the bed he poses, watching Trillious frown and sketch. "Feel free to remain and admire my body as long as you like." Hayden twists at the hips like a glamorous tightrope walker, first left, then right, thickly, imitating heavier wedges. "Shall I lie upon the bed and adopt a languid demeanor for you, darling?"

Poor Trillious, downgraded to one night stand programmed on repeat, shakes their head without ceasing to sketch. "I'm drawing a tarot deck of all my lovers. You're the King of Toilets. Don't change a thing."

"I want to be your toilet. Let's wrap our tongues around each other."

"You can never stop fidgeting long enough for that level of adult commitment. I don't know why you asked me here again just to insist on making fun of me and mocking my very serious art."

Hayden wants to answer with a fart, but he's striving to maintain the illusion that he's not a twelve year old boy beneath his manly body. It is manly, isn't it? Though slender and shaky as a baby bird's leg from his neck to his groin, arms long and white as a swan's throat, it's fundamentally flat in the right places and bulges nicely at the biceps when he wears the right jacket. His father blessed him with a square jaw and a love of good craftsmanship that shows in his careful construction of persona. His mother cursed him with deific genes and a moody heart.

"One of these days, if I'm lucky, I'll learn what it's like to feel the tip of a sharp beak when it enters like a needle and pries the red flaps between my ventricles apart," he says. Hayden hates mother Hera for letting him slip through one of her open wounds with the manifold ease of a hydra in heat. He wishes he'd been man enough as an infant to cause fatal harm in his immortal descent. "You'll never understand. I was born to be adored, a king amongst toilets. A swan amongst songbirds. A muted ace."

Trillious glares at the sketchpad, dissatisfied. "It's always the wrong people who die, isn't it?"

Hayden imagines himself a hysterical hydra, choking with multiple throats. Multiple deaths elude him. Lips pouting, accentuating leftover impressions of acne that pit the edges of his chin and cheeks: "Are you dreaming of my immaculate skin?" Above his wide eyes, forehead scars grow more visible as his hair recedes. Imperfections he embraces, evidence of a body at war. Covered in the skin of Hera's discarded shields, Hayden hopes an ancient leather garment will supplant his youthful glow with battle scars.

Swift corruption is all he can hope for as an idol. Like his dad said, everyone on the scene aged ten years overnight when Ian Curtis died. Music changed. "No balls," his dad summed up in an accent heavy with forbidden elixirs. Secrets upon secrets in the blended cadmium hues. Hayden sneers at his handsome reflection as it wavers from turpentine fumes in the dresser mirror. Ian Curtis shakes pinned on the wall nearby, ecstatic eyes rolled back to whites, a St. Vitus dance beside Hayden's effeminate prance. The slick poster paper cracks with a history of humidity in the vintage fibers. Hayden's dad left him enough money to do something about it. He could get it conservation framed, but that's a sacrilege against the memorial of an honest death that Hayden's not willing to broach.

Death of aesthetics, or monstrous birth? Hayden's birthday is today, May eighteenth. His dad shrugged about the coincidence with closed lips and a knowing look. Their inside joke, though neither one laughed. Hayden kept quiet around his father and listened hard. Sorting evidence from disdain was no simple child's task. It's no surprise *Closer* was the first vinyl Hayden bought with his babysitting money when he was a blushing schoolgirl. Even now it's his go-to album for intoxicated anal sex.

"The suit of toilets encompasses the elements of porcelain and shit." Trillious makes corrections to their drawing. Smudges with a pinky and cocks their head. Gentle frown lines accent the lack of irony. "Contrast informs the proposed deck. The card suits are uncountable: porcelain, attention, dogma, and clarity. In the absence of numeration, the diminutive cards following trumps and royals bear fidelity or opposition to their theme to communicate both rank and import. The Ace is ever-changing, and far from mute. It alters the reading based on whether the interpreter calls it a one or a zero."

"Darling, you said there aren't any numbers. You'll make a terrible witness when they charge you for my crimes. Of course I plan to frame you when I hang." Hayden jabs his tongue out of the side of his mouth in mock strangulation.

Trillious is unmoved. "Numbers exist, with or without the formality of counting. In my deck, suits may appropriate cards from other suits, lending fluidity to divination that some users find vexing. I refuse to corrupt my design. Its ambiguous leanings make it rich in possibility and lore."

They turn the sketchbook to display Hayden's graven image. Frown lines blur into a sly smile over the metal coil connecting pages across the top. One side of the wire is bent at a dangerous angle, its convoluted end unraveled and sharp. Trillious's tone shares a similar path. "I expect to encounter resistance to confusion and uncertainty. It seems no one wants their oracles to be too damn lifelike."

Conscious of the eyes ogling his handsome body, Hayden shifts the cage of skin containing the raw meat of nothingness that feeds the sharks of time inside him. In contrast to the stillness of desire, Hayden yells, twitching. "Well, you certainly can't accuse me of that!"

Always, he feels desire. He twitches faster, growing violent, jerking his shoulders, his knees, and tossing his head atop a cracking neck. He empties out his needs fearfully, like a sea cucumber. Open and erupting, Hayden's a disgorged vessel. A solid lack. Collapsing on the bed, his vocalizations turn asemic.

Trillious tackles Hayden. The sketchpad drops. The page is crushed. Hayden's iconic image mimics his fit. Trillious tries to restrain him and defer the damage of his epileptic dance. Spurious or sincere, a history of black eyes, bruises, and lumps litters the subcutaneous fascia of any fan foolish enough to fall prey to Hayden's drama.

He wrenches away from Trillious. They swing wide over his legs and renew their grip.

Hayden's deep enough in the archive to know this candy wrapper's going straight in the trash the minute he rips it off. Knees slap tender flesh-upholstered bone. Hera slaps the ground and births a new conundrum. Hayden's one of many, monstered out of borrowed parts and bitter vengeance. Excited by his lover's participatory indulgence, he really needs to figure out if this drama has a tragic or comedic arc before they get too close to the ending. Struggling against Trillious, reveling in illness, Hayden garbles out chunks of his unceasing inner monologue. "How dare you claim to care? Pantheon addict. As if I'm your gateway drug to corrupted kings. Drama is my derelict birthright, by all the gods before me."

Pressed on top of Hayden, Trillious giggles, thighs and belly like a sarcophagus full of baked beans, shifting. "But I'm your biggest fan."

"Rotten, rotten; I smell of kings. Kill them all. Kiss off."

"Kiss all kings," and Trillious tries to catch his lips.

Hayden bucks against hips fleshed hysterical as Hera's. He's hard with hate at their wide expanse and forgiving angles, at the loneliness they breed promising all the wrong kinds of pain for a masochist his age. Hayden's worked long and hard to be long and hard. He eschews softness.

Unbalancing his opponent by locking a shin beneath their knee, Hayden grasps their waist and shoulder and pins Trillious on the bed. Hayden's on top, trumpeting desire. "You can't possibly expect me to keep my hands off your throat in this torrid Greek climate, you silly cocksucker."

Hayden tears away lacy packaging and pearls, exposing a creature like a baby rhinoceros that nudges his cunt. Blind with mammalian greed, it seeks a gland to suckle upon. The wrestlers' mutual laughter escalates into breathless screams. Hayden's elbow punctures the portrait. His flying spittle pockmarks the crumpled sketch.

"I can't stand these terrible panties." Hayden intends to roar. Instead he emits a febrile whine that's followed too soon by gushing tears. "How much do you think I can take? I can't handle any of this situation with you. You taste like imported textiles, all musty. Shitty panties like a grandmother, these bouncing clown ears, deceptive frills. Your majestic confluence with ocular anomalies cracks my skull."

The creature between them grunts. Hayden strangles Trillious's bulging throat. "The window dressing you hang on my life, when I'm the thing hanging, I'm what should be hung. I mean hanged. For fuck's sake, I can't even get the past tense of my own suicide correct. No wonder you hate me. You're all I have. I can't live without you. It's disgusting. I've lost control. I'm a fat old hen sewn into a sack of rocks, unable to drown. My god, look at your hideous face."

Trillious gargles. A snakelike tongue protrudes from puffy lips. Foam the color of weak tea gathers. Hayden tastes it, wincing at the smoky rottenness of his recently ingested stench. He sucks hard on the sore tongue and plunges his free hand into Trillious, prodding desperately, hopelessly, pausing long enough to swallow the cascade of moans released from their neck. Hayden shudders. Trillious lies slack as an old shirt.

Pulling out, Hayden tosses away the shredded fabric

he detests. Bright red fingerprints adorn Trillious. Their Adam's apple churns like a conqueror worm. Hayden wipes their face with the back of his fist, smearing more than he cleans.

Pausing with wet knuckles pressed into a soft cheek. "Nothing's real about you. Not your sacrificial panties, or your squirming malachite disguise. You've been a right scheming bitch from the start. You make a satire of love." Jack of all jacks, Hayden's satisfied and disgusted with the mess he's made of Trillious. He's ready to accept his punishment.

He's dying for it.

Reclining in gasps, Trillious coughs out a croak that smooths into husky grunge. "Satyr of love, sinner of all sins, heretic of all heretics. You'll form a hybrid beast of us in ample time. I love you. How I love you. Ribs growing through our skulls like antlers, antlers peeling like cinnamon bark, barking swans swallowing their infinite tails. Feathers of men."

Hayden shakes at the thought of unbridled connection and mutation. "God, can't you just hit me like a normal behemoth?"

His weight evaporates. He digs through the dresser drawer to pilfer his stash for an anchor. He can't stop thinking about someone cutting off his legs and replacing them with overripe carrots. Left a screaming mandrake, sutured back into the earth from which he was torn to embody Hera's revenge, he'd be responsible for more massacres than his current budget allows.

The wall shakes, Ian Curtis always dancing, if anyone still calls it that, marking elaborate time signatures Hayden wants to recreate in his next set. The sensitive man on the poster barely hides the mobled queen beneath. Hayden hears her rustling under the surface of things, threatening to sleepwalk all over his fragile libido. Evidence stains his sheets. Mother Hera haunts the walls, stapled like the plastic barricading a crime scene. Hayden's hardest job is holding her flat.

"Are you okay? That last dose was enough to abort an albatross."

"One of us needs the steel to die like a madman instead of merely dipping our necks in the sludge for a snack. If you hack it off," Hayden says, "let me have it. I see you looking good in taxidermy for the archive. We can start fresh with a new wing."

Palms brushing away strained tears, bile squeezed from an enamored head, Trillious sighs in adulation. "I'm your biggest fan. Trust me, this isn't about him. It never was. I worship you. There's nothing you can do to make me stop loving you, no matter how rotten you pretend to get. Why do you insist on staying in this hole year after year? Let's grow new tails and learn to swim. Let's leave history behind us."

The cracks in the archive are spreading. The walls are as weak as shocked granite, unsuitable for either construction development or common culinary use. A web of flaws unravels the cognitive structures Hayden holds dear. Bare sustenance splayed open in the spider web of cracks, he feels the opposite of a fly, struggling to stay trapped.

Trillious is transformation, stalking him in the tenement halls long before the archive fell out of some demiurge's asshole and landed on earth. They started out young and sneaky, offering to do odd jobs. First it was cheap, then it was free. Somewhere along the way, the sketch pad manifested, Trillious fawning over Hayden's young drunken grace. Drunk on cough syrup in third grade, Hayden mourning his deific predilections. Trillious thrilled, proposed a trade. The attention neutered Hayden for days, but of course he sat for the portraits. Of course he agreed.

Careless beauty sloughs off onto the page. Hayden's old skins pinned to the wall have a bad habit of growing nipples. Pores inflate with glandular excess. Trillious tacks up terrible reminders of what screams beneath Hayden's skin. When the windows are open, Hayden and Hera dance a fluttering paper duet on the walls.

Hayden gulps three tablets dry. Two for expulsion and one for pain. "The king of toilets is working up to one flaming crescendo. I'd birth it in your mouth if I didn't suspect you'd enjoy the experience so much."

"There are infinite ways to fill and be filled."

"I don't want to spoil you, darling. Not just yet. Turn around. Bend over. Don't look at me."

Trillious obeys. "How precious our offspring will be before they drown in menstrual blood, my love. How intrinsically divine. Your perfect jawline, my malachite eyes, and a triton for a tail."

Hayden's angle of approach reveals Trillious gloating

with a murderer's possessive gaze. Their images mate in the mirror like rival songbirds. Hayden's hips flex in parallel aggression with each gluteal thrust. Trillious is bent into a scaffold of indecency, emitting the cyan enzyme of an unwilling slave to biology.

Lilting like a chariot pulled by peacocks, Trillious lectures. "The respective elements of the four suits are air, fire, earth and water." They brush their hairless arms against Hayden's heaving chest, turning tail feathers with gemstone eyes on his motions. "Clarity as water is mutable, evoking its opposite: confusion. You know about that. The duality of the fourth suit creates a fifth ghost suit, if you will. There are no cards for the ghost suit. It is, however, the most important of all five with the corresponding element of ether." Trillious gasps as Hayden heaves into them. "I'm serious. What I mean by all this is that we can be happy together. I've never feared your rages, your moods."

Fascinated by his own transparent skin, Hayden eradicates eye contact. "Isn't there somewhere else you need to be?"

"Are you listening?"

"Don't whine, darling," Hayden says.

How he remains opaque to anyone else is unfathomable. Through his frail tissue paper of epidermis, Hayden watches the writhing black coils of putrefaction that compose his insides. Some are large and thick like rubber hoses, others small and delicate as string. Maggots dance like dollops of static. Multiple roots of abscesses weave a lugubrious pattern of linear uncertainty. The footwork for his partners to follow is complicated and variable. Who Hayden becomes from one day to the next is up for grabs.

A body rots inside him. What a sham, this eternal shifting skin.

Hayden gluts on black market misoprostol and fentanyl.

Another dose, another monstrous birth averted.

Hayden isn't sure why he's so cold or why fucking seems fucking impossible these days. Trillious's voice is indistinct over the loud music and the clamor of the crowd of dance-crazed skins erupting from the walls. Hayden places vinyl on the turntable, fits the needle to the initiatory groove and fades up. From one son to the next, no, he meant to say from one *song* to the next, he considers the hopeful possibility that he's not on stage but actually overdosed and lying cold in bed while Trillious jerks his shoulders with the rhythm of a slam dance hoping he'll revive.

Another day, another suicide. Hayden stains the archive with redundant attempts. The safe spaces he sticks with imprint image after image of crippled gods erupting from concrete. King Hera limps in Hayden's footsteps, following his faun-like outline. Hayden stays one pivot ahead, one kick past parental censure, one stage dive closer to zooicide.

The violence of the dance snaps his head to and fro. When Hayden's neck lolls back, he almost chokes. Trillious tenderly coaxes his face upright next. Holds

Hayden's forehead close to their lips. Whispers. "I worship you. I'm your biggest fan."

"Oh god, that's not creepy at all," Hayden says, but no sound comes out.

For his next set, Hayden has no idea what kind of musical theme to disseminate. Fortunately, the intimate whispering transfers to the speakers, Trillious crosses the dancefloor, and the song doesn't stop. Hayden can't figure out why there's a bed on stage. If he had any energy he'd tell the owner to cut the strobe, too. His retinas throb in syncopated time with the cycles of the turntable and the flashing lights.

Trillious brings him a drink, slinking to the beat and yelling soundlessly across an extended cup. Hayden tastes it and spits. "What the fuck?"

"Everything goes better with hemlock, my love."

Hayden downs the drink in one gulp. "Prove it. The extension of mercy. The dour fountain staunched."

The dim apartment, the bed, the archive: it all flips like a costume change. Every skin on the wall breathes, an outfit wide awake, waiting for a lover to wear it and become fully fleshed. Creatures craving the gift of life. Unwilling idol, hell-bent on sacrifice, Hayden clasps Trillious through the fog of his fast panic gasps. Crushed by the embrace, Trillious murmurs with dry lips into Hayden's straining chest where the stubborn heart of a half-god flutters. "That's more than I could hope for." Trillious presses their face in the softness to the side of Hayden's sternum. "I'm not trying to be ironic. You must know pregnancy increases the risk of thrombosis."

Hayden's unable to draw enough sustenance into his lungs to get more than a word out: "Finish."

Trillious yanks Hayden's belt. It takes extra effort to loosen the clasp with all the weight Hayden's put on. Trillious pulls. The belt slides free like a snake. Trillious drops it on the floor and releases Hayden's gut from his trousers. "It's a question of verisimilitude. How much are you really willing to commit to being plausible? How willing are you to nibble the obscure marrow?"

Hayden's belly swells into a gigantic mound as it slathers out of his fly. "I prefer to wallow in aspiration, lapping at sightless passages." He hiccups. "Oh god, I'm going to be sick."

Carpet smells of unwashed feet mix with dust-clumped desires. The mold growing beneath the surface in the damp foam pad flattens under Hayden's gravid weight. Running and retching, Hayden streams bile across the worn former plush. He slumps shy of the toilet. The mound in his gut kicks. Each hit cracks Hayden's breath into painful splinters.

Codpiece in clown panties, lips like Hera's, pursed, Trillious has grown too massive to fit through the bathroom door. They bellow in a corrugated slur, thickened like chins. "We're eating for two now. No coddling your precious beauty. I've made a fresh portrait of you."

Nurse Trillious extends a new limb which is not an arm or a branch or a corkscrew shaped duck penis that spins with the arrhythmia of St. Vitus dance. It pierces Hayden's belly, shuddering and splattering a new hole. Galvanized, Hayden's spit flows like a river of egg white. The taste of sickness slides freely between his jaws. His guts are slam dancing. Babies bruise tender spleen and cartilage within him. His tumors have finally turned on him, perforating the elastic reproductive organ he thought atrophied. Hayden's abortions fight for an exit wound, devouring their disposable host on the trip down the death canal.

Each turn of the screw brings him closer to sweet release.

Villi escape like errant intentions, paving the way to heavenly unconsciousness. Warm liquids flood Hayden's vast cavity. His reward is within reach. Holy Hera, king of cunts, Trillious nurses a lathered tip into Hayden's mangled slit. In response, Hayden squeezes their prickly skin, milking analgesic pus from engorged pores. The stitches in archival rag barely hold. The nurse costume slips. Breasts between men seek a new bearer. Tissue samples flee below foreign skin.

Once again congealed in blubbery chaos, Trillious punches Hayden in the stomach. "I'm your biggest fan." Their voice doubles in the echoing emptiness of Hayden's abdomen. "I will make my home in you, where your father lies."

The nauseous pain of the gut punch sends Hayden into an aphrodisiac head spin. Revolving waves overcome his resistance. He's blinking in and out, each glimpse of light an overwhelming and unwelcome ping of pleasure.

Trillious drilling: "Jack of all jacks. I'll grant you an exegesis in red."

Describe the vinyl. Needle skips through blackened grooves. Impressions scratch away all cogent sound. Trillious squeezes the satyr to death in the eyeless channel of an overgrown lock. Hayden's orgasm stops when he finds his father shot.

✣

Here his father lies. The blood-pool is sticky where time darkens the liquid, no longer flowing. How long he lay in the apartment alone is a matter for medical examiners to sort. No weapon is located onsite. The bullet pattern indicates an amateur, ruling out a professional hit, although it's everyone's first thought. The rich artist's ties to a certain underworld boss were common lore. They came up in the worker's union together, parted ways in the eighties. Hayden's dad claimed no contact, reports of involvement persisted, part of the man's illustrious mystique. With a cushion of prosperity against serious inquiries, the master craftsman turned master publicist and made the most of notorious rumors.

Hayden wished him dead, of course. The old man was cruel to his untalented mongrel progeny, disdained the proof and product of deific deception. King Hera, Queen of Heaven, meting out her twisted justice of fecundity. She slaps the ground and vomits up a hairball that grows into a bountiful apple orchard. She kicks a brick foundation and the church upon it leaks a pheromone elixir that causes the congregation to ovulate. She grabs a swan by the throat and it farts out a luxuriously endowed trio of dwarves whose laughter impregnates nearby cattle. Suffering from dementia for eons, her doddering fertility rites welcome abusive suitors. Hayden's dad was one fool of many.

But wishes are lies.

When Hayden finds his father shot, the restless bulk of the unmoving masculine body alerts his senses before he sees any blood. The position is all wrong. Lumped over an arm, v-shaped neck thrust back, the garrulous mouth sprouts a slack tongue. Hayden wonders why his socks are wet. He doesn't register how they've soaked up the dead man's blood because he's stood there so long doing nothing.

Hayden can't move. He's trying to figure out why the noise didn't wake him. His room is right above the studio.

Dad lies calm as a bear carcass waiting for flies. Hayden bends and kneels, proving he's capable of moving. Wearing a pink nightgown and white ankle socks, he's baffled by the inordinate silence muffling every sound in the tenement. It's an old building where neighbors grow close like family. In the quiet, Hayden strains an arm over dad's corpulent waistline. His nine-year-old fingers fumble to undo his father's belt. He tries to overlook the modulated mouths of exit wounds and the sensation of a warm turd in the old man's pants. It molds to fit his knee. He yanks the last notch and the clasp comes free.

Hayden slides the belt through the loops and takes it into the kitchen. The water pipe is exposed across the ceiling. Hayden positions a chair beneath it. Still strangely deaf, he can't hear the chalkboard scraping of the legs scoring the floor. It's like being underwater. He hopes he won't float.

Looping the belt over the pipe is easy enough, but

Hayden's long hair gets in the way of hanging. How he hates the old man for forbidding him to cut it. For making him wear skirts. How he hates himself for telling Trillious. Their grandmother kept a pearl handled pistol hidden in the folds of her fat flowered handbag in the suite next door.

The blushing schoolgirl hangs, growing beet red in the face. He watches the warm bear of his father's body growing cold in the corner of his eye. An immortal genepool denies Hayden mimicry of the man he admires.

An end to justice, an unsettling of debts. Silenced by slashes as drastic as the belt, Hayden takes refuge. In music. In corrugated silence. In archetypal lies. Nine or nine-hundred years old, Hayden deviates into helpless rebellion. As Trillious guts him, Hayden realizes the master plan for his next set: three turntables, one dog.

Johnny Thunders live. Slumping, slurring, an intoxicated godhead. Message undermined. The variant is the position, the choice. Will you take the stage or feed it your wonder until the well runs dry? Sid Vicious next, with impossible vocals like a deprived child. Michael Gira wins with hopeless gravel drone metamorphosing into an altered verse: "And now I want to be your god."

Words of an idiot.

Slumping in undone innards on the bathroom floor. Hanging from the kitchen water pipe overnight. Teaching a wound to speak. Too much time to contemplate Hera's glory as a crust. She forms from his suicides, matron dissected in reverse. Wallpaper tears where the nine-year-old hangs without hanging, chokes without choking. Strangled into silence, the child helpless as

Hera peels flesh long trapped in battlements and fills up her lumpy form. She steps, unsteady, ripping out doll stitches, sword lowered, poised for havoc, for gutting guilty swans, for plucking pearls from a murderer's eyes. Fragile in strength, the blind goddess wobbles as much as she kills.

"Uh, secular," Hayden moans. The warning is explicitly missed.

H ayden cries.

"I'm dreaming, I'm dying, this is an overdose. I'm hallucinating my next suicide. This can't be real, it can't." But it is real. As real as Trillious ripping into Hayden's unwanted organ, thus solving the problem of its unwanted contents.

Hayden hating, emptied of erotic inhabitants with his womanhood spread. It spins Hayden's head. Like a record baby right round. His wound whispers and weeps with the beat. Thighs tensed, back arched, ass flexed, Hayden's hollows howl.

Trillious quenching their thirst for impalement and repetition. "I'll do anything for you."

Distended and retracted in wet flaps, Hayden's begging for the kid to see King Hera hulking behind them. Taking in their sounds and returning his own, he's dreaming of a fiendish diagnostic idol, of asylum with a hemlock-cured misanthrope, buzz buzz into the secular modification connector. "I'm worthless," Hayden groans.

Trillious says, "Try to be more careful. Next time you're going to hemorrhage or get an infection."

"I hate you."

"I worship you."

"Don't leave me. How could you leave me?"

Guilty as a swan, Hayden hides trembling in the archive as King Hera descends, clavicles cocked. She of the ready sword and imploded eyes, she of the suckling ragged skins and shredded clown disguise, she of memory loss and staggering idiot vengeance. She, King Hera, Spring Virgin, Summer Mother, Autumn Crone, Winter King, totters from Olympus to fuck another swan and be fucked. The mythic circle of immortal life, the fallacy of return, and the corruption of sickly gods. Hayden sees her face in the mirror behind Trillious.

Bound downward, ancient harridan King Hera slaps the ground and births an infinite number of roaring reiterations of her husk, her cunt, her mane. Gathered and tethered, Trillious falling prey, pickling into a permanent girl, joining the shriveled imitations lining the archive, lost dolls and mutated suitors, fans and foes trapped within King Hera's skin.

Hayden can't stand it. Not again.

Mother Hera mocks Hayden's desire with Trillious limp in her grip. This time, Hayden doesn't turn away. He shoves his unrenewed virginity between captor and slave. Trillious is freed from Hera's all-consuming stitches in a tumble of bull skulls and cuckoo feathers. Parts of Hayden sloughed off in passion leave him like ready traitors. The unwholesome effort overthrows his magical biology. Trillious loses sight of the collapsed idol bleeding out on the crowded dance floor. Their offspring scatter.

Hayden faces Hera alone. For a moment he feels more like a real man than ever. With toxic castration, with quivering archive, with dreams of defeat, with carnivorous bravado, with monstrous birth from monstrous birth, with monstrous birth from monstrous loins, he screams at Trillious, and Hera's nipples wither. "I am what I devour, I am what I own, love me, admire me, I hate you, you cocksucker. I can't live without you. Don't leave me. I love you. I've lost control."

# THE FRUIT OF A BARREN TREE
## - SAM RICHARD

I hadn't touched that revolver in years. So long that I wasn't quite sure it was still here; hoping that I hadn't forgotten I'd moved it from the crumbling shoe box on the bedroom closet shelf, where it sat for years behind all the old photo albums. All of Melissa's old pictures. Mementos from a dead life; from a dead bride.

The revolver had belonged to my father. Something we found in that same ancient shoe box, sitting underneath his bed, when we went through the house after he died. He spent his life struggling with depression and anxiety, though those were never terms in his vocabulary. When we found it, I wondered how many drunken nights he had cradled it while holding back tears, how many times he placed it against his temple, willing himself to pull the trigger. At least he made his exit less messy for all of us, opting to hang himself instead. It felt like some kind of horrible silver lining.

Suicide was the only estate I was due, or so I told myself. I reasoned that the 20th anniversary of my wife's death was as appropriate a day as any, so I woke up early, made breakfast, and headed to the closet to get the old man's gun, provided it was still there.

Digging toward the back of the shelf, my elbow knocked a few photo albums to my feet, sending loose pictures scattering across the bare, wooden floor. It felt improper to die in a messy house, something about leaving things unfinished was wrong at its core, so I got down on my aching knees to gather them.

Most were pictures of us when we were in our first couple of years of marriage. Before the cancer had worn her body down. Shots of us smiling with friends at parties, polaroids from a road trip we took through the south, wedding pictures. I fought tears as I looked at them, though I was also smiling. So much happiness and potential. An entire lifetime together ahead of us, or so we thought.

What a life we would have lived had her cells not begun to grow irregularly. One of warmth and joy, one of struggle, too--no doubt--but not the struggle of the past two decades. I spent that time trying to find something, someone, who could help take the pain away. Maybe someone who could stand in for Melissa, but that was a fool's errand. Or even just someone to distract me from the emptiness rotting away in my heart. But all that I found was more loneliness, more suffering. A whole big world full of people, and none of them her.

As I collected the scattered pictures, one stuck out to me. A photo of a large mushroom at the trunk of a gnarled tree. She had taken it one warm summer after-noon when we had just started dating. Seeing the image triggered memory after memory of that day. We went to the Natural History Museum, then to a mall for shitty pretzels, before ending at the Quaking Bog, one of her favorite parks in the city, where she had taken the photo.

The memories felt tactile in my mind, like I could reach through them and touch her face. Like I could jump into them and warn these two young people the misery that awaited them. But I fought against that, the idea of placing that burden on their backs was too much to bear. I wanted to let those people we once were have their time before life turned sour.

Staring at the mushroom, I wanted to hold some of that joy and hope again, even just for a second. Melissa loved the bog, loved the natural world. If I could experi-ence that with her again, maybe the vast expanses of nothing after death wouldn't feel so bad. Maybe I could bring that one piece of joy with me. So I headed to the bog in search of the mushroom, or at least the tree that loomed above it. I hoped I could find some peace there. Peace before the silence.

The gun could wait.

Once I arrived, a tangle of dirt paths leading into different sections of the park caused me some confusion; something that always happened to me at that park. Eventually I found a sign that pointed me in the right direction. Despite the chilly fall weather, a moisture grew in the air the closer I got to the bog.

Walking along the plastic docks, the crisp air smelled of decay and earthiness. I replayed that day in my mind,

Melissa walking beside me, our hands locked together. She told me about the bog, about the specific mineral-less conditions of the water. About the tangle of moss, vine, and root structures that create the bog surface. She told me about how some of the Native tribes in the region thought it was a sacred place. And how some of the early European settlers avoided it, thinking it was a cursed and alien region.

We talked about what it would be like to stumble upon the bog while walking through the wilderness. If you didn't know about it, or about bogs at all, what kind of reaction that might evoke in someone. As I walked, I remembered the way she laughed, not just on that day, but all the time. I remembered how excited she was when she spotted the mushroom behind some of the other growth. How in love with the crooked tree she was.

You aren't supposed to walk on the bog surface, signs are posted everywhere warning visitors to stay on the path, but she couldn't help herself. I watched her sneak off the path to take a photo of the mushroom, of the strange tree. I couldn't tell what variety the fungi was, knowing little of mycology myself, but she knew all about it, telling me facts as she took photos.

When I reached that same area, or what I remembered as being roughly the same area, I, too, broke the rules. No part of me expected that mushroom to still be there, all these years and seasons later, and especially since there was such a chill in the air, but I hoped at least the tree was still standing. Having that connection with her one more time meant the whole world to me. To stand where she stood, to experience the beauty of nature the way she saw it, just one more time.

Stepping over the small railing, my heart beat faster and harder, knowing I might be seen. I felt like a child trying to skip school on a warm spring day, unable to hold out for summer vacation a second longer. The intensity of this fear of getting caught made no sense to my rational brain. The worst they could do would be to ask me to leave the park, but I was also afraid knowing that if they did stop me, I wouldn't be able to visit this spot that meant so much to her; that now held a sense of sacredness to me.

The fear became all the more absurd once I reminded myself that I was likely entirely alone, probably in the whole park area, even. I hadn't seen anyone at all while I walked to the bog from my car.

A woven tapestry of plant-life was uneasy under my feet, shifting around me as I sunk slightly with each step. In my memories, the area hadn't been too far off the path, but far enough that she had to walk a bit while I kept an eye out for anyone who might chastise her. After a few shaky steps, I reached a spot past some of the more dense, browning foliage that had grown over the years and spotted a large, crooked tree.

It appeared to be the place, though I knew I would never be one-hundred percent certain. Looking down, to the spot where the mushrooms sat, I was shocked to see a few small, dirt-streaked stalks poking through the mossy surface. They were white with a subtle blue beneath them and stood in an almost triangular pattern.

The mushroom Melissa had been so enamored with

was significantly bigger and rounder than these and I wondered if they were newly sprouted stems of the same variety, much younger and therefore smaller than the one in her photo.

They looked cold and weather-beaten. The spot was imbued with a special warmth, knowing she had stood here, knowing we had spent the day at a spot that made her so overwhelmingly happy. Wanting to somehow mark the occasion, to acknowledge the force that had brought me here, I thought I should at least pay this fungus some kind of acknowledgment.

Bending down on one knee, my joints creaking in pain, I touched my finger to one of the small outgrowths. The surface was gritty and cold, but harder than I expected to be. I assumed it would be at least mildly spongy, not the almost silicon texture and buoyancy that it held.

There was also something coming out of them that I hadn't noticed immediately, like a small sliver crested in dirt. At first, I thought it was a piece of wood, but then I wondered how and why they all had them. It was only after studying them for several seconds that my mind turned over on itself. I wasn't touching a mushroom at all.

They were human fingers coming up through the surface of the bog.

I fell back onto the moss as panic scratched at my chest. Freezing water soaked through my jacket and sweatshirt, chilling me as I tried to wrangle myself back to my feet. Time slowed down, a sensation I recalled all too well from the day Melissa breathed her last breath.

I tried to calm myself, to not let this pull me into a PTSD spiral, but I couldn't get that moment out of my mind; I also couldn't rid myself of the thought that I was standing over a body. Centering myself, as best as I could, I struggled to figure out what I should do, but all I could see was Melissa's lifeless face staring vacantly at the ceiling, her light having been extinguished.

In a panic at the thought that this person may still be alive, I started tearing at the bog surface, trying to free them from the floating tangle of moss, vines, and roots. As I did, the ground beneath me began to buckle and shift, allowing more glacial water to lap at my already frigid legs.

Once I had moved enough of the surface out of the way, I grabbed the stranger's hand and tried to wrench them out of the water as swiftly as I could, my feet becoming submerged in the murky, penetrating deluge. They barely shifted, likely caught on something. Knowing the ground beneath me would give at any moment, I had no time to perform a surgical maneuver to dislodge them from whatever they were tethered to, so I wrenched again, this time with all the force my aching back, inflamed joints, and sinking feet could muster.

A subdued snapping sound rang under the water and they were now free as I pulled them onto the surface. The ground continued to break beneath us as I walked, so as quickly as I could, I dragged them to the plastic walkway that serpentined through the bog. Shivering in my soaked clothes, I bent down to check for a pulse, and likely administer CPR.

But the face staring back at me was a face I hadn't seen for over 20 years; a face seared into my memory that I would never forget. A face I would never stop loving.

It was Melissa.

There was no breath. From either of us.

She had that same vacant, glassy look in her brown eyes, though they were now marred by a reddish-brown discoloration. Her skin was flat white with the same subtle blue that was upon her fingers. The rest of her was also covered in patches and streaks of mud.

At the center of her chest, there was a protrusion. In my state of shock, I couldn't figure out what it was at first until I realized that it was a root stabbing into her heart. I felt oddly comfortable allowing my trauma to distance what was happening in front of me and enter into the role of amateur medical investigator. But my emotional dissociation was short lived as I started getting dizzy and thought I might pass out.

Trying my best to breathe through it, tears of bafflement trickled onto the plastic dock below us, despite my best efforts to fight them. A flare of anger rose in my stomach and up my chest. I had already endured so much, and now the universe decided that I was to be confronted by an impossible encounter with my late wife, 20 years after her death and cremation, but that in it she would still be dead.

It was so cruel.

I gripped the root stabbing into her chest with my numb hands and pulled as hard as I could. A wet crunch came with it as it separated from her, lifting her body up slightly as it dislodged.

What should have been a wound was a perfectly neat opening. The flesh and muscle folded away from the hole, which was filled with a tangle of roots. A shudder went through me as I kneeled over her and cried.

Faint voices echoed through the bog. They were light and conversational. Blood pounded in my veins at the thought of being seen with this... Of being seen with her. There was no way to explain it. There was no rational universe in which any of this made sense. She may have been dead, but she was still my wife. Consumed by panic and shock, picked her up, and carried her through the bog and out to my car, trying my best to take a route as far away from the quickly loudening voices as possible.

Setting her down in the back seat, I took off my soaking coat and draped it over her before getting in and cranking the heat as high as it could go. The drive home was full of confusion and anxiety, as I grappled with what had happened; with the fact that my long dead wife's corpse was somehow in the backseat of my car, looking like she had somehow been reborn and died again. A version of her from before the cancer. Not worn by illness and chemo like she had been at the time of her death.

Everything was a blur and I'm amazed that I didn't crash into anyone before I pulled into the garage. Still shivering, I did my best to cradle Melissa in my arms and carry her into the house. Laying her on the couch and draping her in a blanket, I went into the bedroom and changed into warm, dry clothes.

I then brought her into the bathroom to wash the dirt off of her body. The clean mineral smell of the bog was starting to wear off and her flesh now held a pallor, grey cast. A faint sweet odor hung thick in the air around her as I gently set her into the steamy, running water. Much of the dirt fell off upon contact and floated to the porcelain bottom of the clawfoot tub.

Love radiated towards her in a way that I had forgotten even existed within me. It was the sensation I once had all the time, before she was gone. I'd gotten brief and subtle hits of it over the years since her death, but those had mostly faded with age and distance. Like a callous had slowly grown over that part of me.

I still couldn't believe any of it. I wondered if I was dreaming, but things had been too linear for that, so I knew it was real. Another sensation I had previously experienced; both upon hearing the news of her cancer and then again on her eventual passing.

I drained the dirty water and used the shower hose attachment to get the remaining muck off of her. I tried to clear out the hole in her chest, expecting blood and other bodily fluids to pour out, but only dirty water came.

How long had she been in there? How was any of this even possible?

I wondered if there was something still lodged in her chest. Maybe a root cluster got in there or I accidentally pressed her into a loose part of the tree when I pulled her out and that's what got stuck. Reaching my hand in, I grabbed a hold of one of the thicker stems and pulled, hoping to dislodge the whole mess. The root flexed with my tug, but didn't move much beyond that, so I tried again.

This time I tried to use my knee as leverage, bracing it against her shoulder and pulling with greater strength. There was a loud snapping sound and some dark fluid ran out of the fissure in her chest. Touching it with my fingertips, it was gritty and cold, like mud.

It was also dripping from her nose.

For fear of hurting her further, I stopped what I was doing and wiped the mud off of her face, the dams in my eyelids threatening to break as I gently cleaned her. The bath had mildly warmed her body, but she was still radiating clammy cold from her depth. I wrapped her in a towel and brought her back to the living room, set her on the couch, and wondered what the fuck was even happening.

Going to the kitchen, I grabbed an old, dusty bottle of Laphroaig from the cupboard above the refrigerator. Never one for much drinking, I'd held onto it over several years as it had been a birthday present. I think I'd drank from it once, probably around when I got it.

Melissa's favorite blue coffee mug was sitting where it always had in the glassware cupboard. It was the only cup that made any sense to drink from, so I poured a heavy splash in the mug and swallowed the whole thing in one go.

The smokiness was overwhelming, like drinking an ashtray, and the alcohol fumes burned my nose. I suddenly remembered both why I rarely drank and why I'd only drank from this particular bottle once. But the sudden influx of alcohol warmed my trembling guts and brought me a new sense of calm. I poured another and tried to drink it faster, but this one got the better of me and I choked a bit, coughing some of it up.

Tears brimmed in my eyelids and I decided to not resist, so down my cheeks they dripped. I had come so far in my grief journey. To the point where I thought I was prepared for anything. And here I was, confronted by something that there was no guidebook--internal or otherwise--could help steer me through. Or so I told myself, trying to forget what I had intended earlier that morning.

A part of me wondered if I had snapped, if something inside had finally gone over the deep end. This could not be. Things like this didn't happen. Was it all some big misunderstanding? Had I simply found a corpse that looked vaguely like Melissa and my brain forced the parts to fit for some strange reason? I grasped at straws, wondering if I should call someone like the police or a psychiatrist, but then decided that I should go and make sure that the body was even there, that I hadn't somehow imagined or created this whole thing in an elaborate fit of mania. Though, in my heart, I knew she would be right where I left her. The touch of her skin, it was all too real.

Before I could check on her, still lost in this serpentine labyrinth of contradictory thoughts and impulses, while pouring another drink, I heard a loud splintering coming from the living room. Scotch still in hand, I ran to her and saw a part of her, something beneath the towel, trying to push the towel off. Hesitantly, I removed the bristly fabric and there was a large expansion growing outward from the roots inside her chest.

It was a small tree, maybe a foot in length, with a few wispy branches. About halfway up it, there was a small fracture, giving it a slight slump.

Her skin was significantly more green, even in the relative dim of the sole table lamp and a fetid odor filled the air. At the trunk of the tiny tree, where it met the hole in her chest, reddish mud oozed down her torso and dripped onto the floor.

I couldn't help myself. I walked over to her and touched the newly sprouted tree. It was cold like her. Looking down the stalk, into the cavity in her chest, I could see that it was connected to the tangle of roots inside of her. At first I thought it was the low light, but the roots appeared to be slowly moving. I turned a lamp on to get a better look, downing the liquor, and got as close as I could to make sure my eyes weren't playing tricks on me. Some roots languidly swam around in the ossein chamber of her rib cage, others seemed to dig deeper, boring further into her body.

Gazing into the hole filled with moving roots, the scotch caught up with me and the room began to spin. The whole affair suddenly felt farcical, absurd, and I couldn't help but laugh. I leaned back on the couch, next to my wife and her tree, and laughed and laughed and laughed. The only thing that stopped the laughter was the eventual tears. A tremor went through me and I couldn't stop crying, couldn't stop asking the universe why this had happened; couldn't stop asking Melissa why she was here.

At some point I blacked out, or passed out, or simply fell asleep, because the next thing I remember was waking up to the morning sun glaring through the window and a monstrous headache. I was in such a state and in surveying the room for damages, I was startled by the sight of Melissa. She was still resting on the couch, but the tree growing out of her had more than tripled in size. Wide branches spotted with tiny buds filled the air above the sofa and the trunk was now strong and thick as my fist.

Melissa looked tattered and worn, her flesh was shiny, blistered. Over the course of the night her eyes had sunken into their sockets and all the skin on her face had grown thin, like it had been stretched too tightly over her skull. And then the odor hit me.

A vile, rotting stench filled the room and my already nauseous stomach started having a fit. I ran outside as quickly as I could, hoping to save myself the mess. Luckily the fresh air helped and I was able to breathe it down, though the light breeze did nothing for my pounding head.

Sitting on my front steps, I sat and cried, wondering what it was that I was even doing. Wondering how I had gotten here at all. In the harsh light of morning, none of this made any sense, though it hadn't prior either, I forced myself to remember. It was like I had been a passenger on a trip I never agreed to, though that hardly explained anything.

With my head in my hands, I asked Melissa for some help, something I had done often through the years. I didn't know what I thought about the afterlife, opting more to believe that anything, even eternal silence, was possible, but that never stopped me from asking her for help, or for guidance, or even for love. I don't know that it ever really worked, but I liked talking with her. It made our connection feel real still, even though she was gone.

Or, even though she had been gone, at least.

I considered simply burying her, the tree sprouting from her could stand as a reminder, a gravestone of sorts. But that felt weird, as she already had a gravestone. Her body was already resting, though in an ashen state, at the cemetery not far out of town.

Maybe they didn't cremate her, though, I wondered. Perhaps something had happened and she had been dumped in the bog. But that made less sense. How had her body been so pristine, so like she was before the cancer.

I was losing it. None of it could be real. No amount of rationalizing what had occurred could make plausible the fact that my long-dead and cremated wife's body was in my living room with a tree sprouting from its heart. Not even booze helped with that.

Trying my best to gather my thoughts, I forced myself back into the foul smelling house. I needed to make sure I wasn't crazy. That this was truly Melissa. I thought that maybe the scotch had warped my view, that perhaps it was truly all some kind of crazy dream, but when I walked into the living room, I was reminded that it was all too real.

Melissa had further decayed, her skin was now pulling back from the bone. It looked like ancient, brittle leather. Her bones were dusty beneath. Her tree was so large that it pressed against my ceiling. Branches were sloped downward, labored under the weight of their fruit, which were red-brown and sticky looking. Honey-like liquid slowly dripped off of them onto the carpet and sofa below, creating an irregular ring around the tree; around Melissa.

She was a sacrifice upon an altar; an offering in a ritual circle.

I looked deeply into her sunken eyes. Her face was radiating with love and beauty. There was something so comforting about the way her lips peeled back from her mouth, exposing grey, gnarled teeth. She was as beautiful as she was the day we first met, as the day we were married, as the day she died.

Reaching out to touch her cheek, a flicker of recognition came across her face and her eyes moved slightly; her opaque, reddened pupils dilated as she looked at me.

She was alive.

The tree shuddered as I touched her, sending more of her treacle splattering to the floor and onto the two of us. There were so many things I needed to say to her, but I could conjure none of them. Pressing our faces close together, I went to kiss her, but before I could, she opened her mouth and mud poured out.

Her eyes pleaded with me, not to end her pain or suffering, but like she needed something from me. A look I remembered all too well from her time in the hospital. I struggled to put my ear as close to her mouth as I could, hoping to hear words escape her mud-caked lips.

"Eat the fruit."

It was so quiet and strained, I wasn't sure that I heard her right, that first time.

"Eat the fruit and be one with me..."

And then the brief and subtle light in her eyes went out, for the final time.

Tears evacuated my eyes with ardor and my heart crushed to dust under its own weight. Having Melissa, and watching her die, again, was far too much to bear. I cursed myself for being too cowardly to go through with my suicide attempt earlier, that I had allowed myself to be distracted by nostalgia and grief. I didn't think I could endure this again.

I thought about dad's gun.

But Melissa's voice also rang in my head, her final act; her final request. She hadn't gotten one of those in the hospital. We knew it would be soon, but there's never enough time. And one morning she was simply here and then gone. So much time spent agonizing over it, in some ways hoping that she could finally get relief, and when it came I felt nothing but guilt and isolation. I needed to at least grant her final request.

Standing on shaky legs, I reached up and grabbed one of the pieces of fruit. Its syrup was sticky and thick like molasses, cooling my hand as I plucked it from the branch. The deep smell of rot had been replaced with the leathery, lilac scent of styrax, which calmed my trembling nerves.

I brought the fruit to my mouth, inhaling the sweet aroma. Before I bit into it, I looked down at Melissa. She was little more than a skeleton now. What little skin she still had was now papery and coated in dust.

The tangle of roots in her chest wrapped through and around all of her bones. One root was around her neck, its end peeking through her open mouth. Another encircled most of her spine. Wherever there was bone, there was root.

I stifled a sob and unceremoniously took a bite of the increasingly slimy fruit. It tasted of perfume and decay. Pulling it away from my mouth, the inside was black as tar and shimmering with oil. The foul taste made me gag, but I forced myself to swallow the chunk whole. I would not leave her final request unfinished.

The bilious fruit slid down my throat, burning my sinuses with the smell of putrefaction. When it finally reached my stomach, it seemed to expand, making me uncomfortably full.

I was also exhausted, not just emotionally, but physically.

The morning sun called to me and I lazily headed out into my back yard. Finding a nice spot of grass, not too close to anything else, I laid down, figuring it would be a nice place for a nap. My stomach groaned and the discomfort increased until it reached a point of numbness.

Everything was so peaceful and nice, as I closed my eyes.

I only wish Melissa was here to enjoy it with me.

## ABOUT THE STORIES
### REFLECTIONS AND CONTEXT FROM THE AUTHORS

### God of the Silvered Halls
Roland Blackburn

What's the old phrase? *Live fast, die young, and leave a beautiful corpse?*

We've all known pretty things that were rotten to core, and when Sam pitched the idea for the anthology, it interlocked perfectly with the fragment of an idea I'd had tossing around about a cadaver with an unusual tattoo. What you put into your body really is what you get out of it, and with the lurking cliché right there about *skin deep,* the rest of the concept just fell into place.

The story itself went about half a dozen ways and a number of frenzied internet searches before it reconciled itself into this final form. In the end, it settles on the universal fear that our bodies will betray us, though admittedly most of us aren't worried about our tum-tums in quite the same way as our protagonist.

### Threnody
Jo Quenell

This story is based off of the song "Funeral" by Phoebe Bridgers. I love the idea of writing pieces influenced by music, and I've been forming this story in my head for the past few years since first hearing this beautiful, haunting song. I'm grateful for the opportunity to finally get it on paper.

Being transgender means often having to live with the memories and guilt of your former self. This isn't a trans story, but it is an earnest attempt to write about living with that weight. This was also my first time writing something that might be considered quiet fiction; I don't think I've ever written a story before that doesn't include the word "blood." Wild. A huge thank you to Sam Richard for once again believing in me and giving me a chance.

## The Queen of the Select
### Katy Michelle Quinn

When given the prompt of beautiful/grotesque, my mind immediately went to Poppy Z. Brite's *Exquisite Corpse*. I wanted to capture a little bit of what he captured in that novel. Sick pleasure taken from a dead or dying body. Tying queerness in (like I always do), I connected this feeling with the self-shaming lust often felt for trans women and their bodies. Finding a body beautiful, but feeling gross about it. Once I had that idea, I tied it into this fictional upper-crust rendering of the rich and privileged who gather to get their yucks at the expense of others. And of course, a violent, closeted, COVID-denying cop provided the perfect depiction of what bastards those sort can be.

# Swanmord

Joanna Koch

I'm always up for an ekphrastic dare. It gets creepy sometimes, though, you know? For instance, I dreamed about writing this statement about Swanmord before the story was written. Not the statement you're reading; the one I deleted a moment ago. I had to stop. It gave me the shivers. I had the dream years ago, before I was a writer, back when I thought I was going to be an artist. Joke's on me. Turns out I don't make the images. I just interpret them.

They're out there everywhere, and also, if you believe certain theorists, inside of us, in the very structure of our DNA. We're made of myths. We construct our reality from raw scraps of arcane lore strewn throughout our biology. Sometimes, biology can be our enemy.

The prompt image for Swanmord irritates the hell out of me. I needed a bigger context to cope with those terrible panties (as the King of Toilets would say), so I did a ridiculous amount of research on the artist Zdzisław Beksiński. I learned that he was murdered by a neighbor (I think), and that his son was a well-known DJ who committed suicide (I think) and was obsessed (possibly) with Ian Curtis. The reason I'm not sure about all this is that I deliberately read articles one time and forbade myself from fact checking. This is fiction, after all, and surrealism, and in Swanmord I wanted to explore nonsense, gaps, and disorder. Those mundane, mysterious errors that (maybe, please, Hera willing) can open larger vistas of the Mystical in the most carnal places in our lives.

### The Fruit of a Barren Tree
Sam Richard

Like nearly everything I've written over the recent years, *The Fruit of a Barren Tree* is really about the death of my wife. For me, the core of the story is about hope that there's still some eerie beauty and cosmic mystery in the world, even when things are at their bleakest; even when one may be considering checking out early.

Granted, I write horror, so perhaps in this instance, the hope is misplaced and the mystery is somehow worse than the already terrible reality that preceded it, but at least there was a hint of something beautiful, before it all rotted away in front of us; before we we were taken by the horror.

## ABOUT THE AUTHORS

**Roland Blackburn** is a father, IPA enthusiast, and the author of *The Flesh Molder's Love Song*, *Marmalade*, and *Seventeen Names for Skin*. He lives in Troutdale with his wife, children, and two dogs. While he didn't find the recipe in a mortuary, he can still whip up one mean jambalaya.

**Jo Quenell** lives in Washington State and writes. Her short fiction has appeared in *Bleak Friday*, *Zombie Punks Fuck Off*, *Lazermall*, *Dark Moon Digest*, and elsewhere. Her debut novella, *The Mud Ballad*, was released by Weirdpunk books in Spring 2020. She teaches middle school through a computer screen, which is scarier than fiction.

**Katy Michelle Quinn** is a queer transwoman who writes weird and weepy horror-adjacent fiction. Her two books thus far are *Girl in the Walls* from CLASH Books and *Winnie* from Eraserhead Press, and her stories have been featured in *Lazermall* and *The New Flesh*. Currently, she inhabits the forests of Cascadia with her partner and their cats Indiana, Cricket, and Widdershins.

**Joanna Koch** writes literary horror and surrealist trash. Author of *The Wingspan of Severed Hands* and *The Couvade*,

Joanna is a Shirley Jackson Award finalist whose short fiction can be found in *Year's Best Hardcore Horror 5*, *Not All Monsters*, and *The Big Book of Blasphemy*. Find Joanna at horrorsong.blog and on Twitter @horrorsong.

**Sam Richard** is the author of *Sabbath of the Fox-Devils* and the Wonderland Award-Winning Collection *To Wallow in Ash & Other Sorrows*. He is co-editor of the Splatterpunk Awards Nominated Anthology *The New Flesh: A Literary Tribute to David Cronenberg* and the owner of Weirdpunk Books. Widowed in 2017, he slowly rots in Minneapolis with his dog, Nero.

*The Wingspan of Severed Hands* by Joanna Koch

Three Women, One Battle. A world gone mad. Cities abandoned. Dreams invade waking minds. An invisible threat lures those who oppose its otherworldly violence to become acolytes of a nameless cult. As a teenage girl struggles for autonomy, a female weapons director in a secret research facility develops a living neuro-cognitive device that explodes into self-awareness. Discovering their hidden emotional bonds, all three unveil a common enemy through dissonant realities that intertwine in a cosmic battle across hallucinatory dreamscapes. Time is the winning predator, and every moment spirals deeper into the heart of the beast.

*Seventeen Names for Skin* by Roland Blackburn

After a cancer diagnosis gives her six-months to live, Snow
Turner does what any introverted body-piercer might: hire a
dark-web assassin and take out a massive life insurance policy to
help her ailing father. But when a vicious attack leaves her all
too alive and with a polymorphic curse, the bodies begin
stacking up. As the insatiable hunger and violent changes
threaten to consumer her, she learns that someone may still be
trying to end her life. Can Snow keep her humanity intact, or
will she tear everything she loves apart?

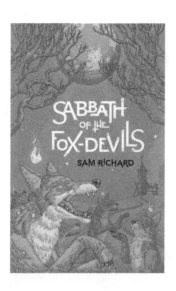

*Sabbath of the Fox-Devils* by Sam Richard

After learning about the existence of a powerful grimoire through a cartoon, 12-year-old Joe is determined to find it and change his lot in life. But in doing so, he'll also uncover a local priest's dark secret and how it may be connected to Joe's brother abruptly leaving town five years ago.

Part homage to the small-creature horror films of the 80s (*Ghoulies*, *Gremlins*, *The Gate*) and part Splatterpunk take on a Goosebumps book, *Sabbath of the Fox-Devils* is a weird, diabolical coming-of-age horror story of self-liberation in an oppressive religious environment set during the Satanic Panic. Prepare your soul to revel in the darkness.

"Light the black candles and invert the cross as Sam Richard conjures a coming-of-age story of Satanic panic, creature carnage, and blasphemous terror!"

— RYAN HARDING (*GENITAL GRINDER*)

*The Mud Ballad* - Jo Quenell

NEVER BE ALONE AGAIN

In a dying railroad town, a conjoined twin wallows in purgatory for the murder of his brother. A disgraced surgeon goes to desperate ends to reconnect with his lost love. When redemption comes with a dash of black magic, the two enter a world of talking corpses, flesh-eating hogs, rude mimes, and ritualistic violence.

"Jo Quenell's debut novella explores both regret and connection in the weirdest and wildest ways possible. Good times!"

— DANGER SLATER (*IMPOSSIBLE JAMES)*